JANET McNEILL
My Friend
Specs McCann

JANET McNEILL
My Friend
Specs McCann

POOLBEG

First published in mcmlv by
Faber and Faber Ltd

This edition in 1995 by
Poolbeg Press Ltd,
Knocksedan House,
123 Baldoyle Industrial Estate,
Dublin 13, Ireland

A catalogue record for this book is available from the British Library.

ISBN 1 85371 537 9

Cover illustration by Jon Berkeley
Cover design by Poolbeg Group Services Ltd
Set by Poolbeg Group Services Ltd in Garamond 10.5/4
Printed by The Guernsey Press Ltd,
Vale, Guernsey, Channel Islands.

For Frances and Connor

Contents

1. In the Swim   1

2. An Unnatural History Story   12

3. Specs by Moonlight   21

4. Specs and that Awful Dog   31

5. Specs and the White Rabbit   40

6. Giving the Bird the Bird   49

7. For Services Rendered   58

8. A Question of Gravity   68

9. Specs and the Cuckoo Clock   78

10. Specs's Midsummer Night's Dream   86

11. Specs's Uncle Ephraim   95

1

In the Swim

Did you see the photograph in last Thursday's paper of the winners in our School Swimming Sports? If you did, the huge cup like a vegetable dish in the middle of the picture was the plum of the prizes – the Open Championship – and the ugly little fellow holding it is my friend, Specs McCann. The cup is so big you can't see much of Specs – only his glasses and his grin. The other chaps in the photo are looking a bit solemn and haughty (like a team of performing seals after their act) but Specs is grinning his head off, and I'll tell you why.

We rather pride ourselves on swimming at our school. Of course the school's right slap on the coast, but it's a nasty coast for bathing, with sharp rocks and tricky tides, so we have the water piped up to the school baths. Some Old Boy left a packet to build them, and they've certainly got everything that baths ought to have. The School Sports are held towards the end of the summer term, so of course all term the water in the baths is churned up nearly to boiling with chaps practising. Specs McCann is small for his age – we were both thirteen last Christmas – but he swims jolly well, and by

1

half-term he seemed on top of his form. Of course the big chaps had the advantage over him; he'd be nipping along like a sardine in a hurry, and they'd be hauling themselves through the water like great whales, each pull taking them as far as two pulls took Specs. It was to be a long half-term, Thursday evening to Monday – and everyone was going home. But on Wednesday, Specs got word that his sister had got measles – the kid had had all summer to take measles, but she had to choose that week-end – so Specs had to stay on at school. I was fed up too, because Specs' mother had written to ask me to go home with him, and it would have been a bit of a spree. You see I live at school, my father's the headmaster.

Anyhow, there we were, stuck at school like two jellyfish when the tide goes out, just Matron and a couple of the maids were left – my father was away in Dublin, but I stayed, of course, because of Specs.

Well, we thought we'd make the best of a bad job and put in some swimming practice. I'm no earthly good at swimming – Specs says it's only my big ears that keep my head above water – but it's company for Specs. We spent Friday morning at the baths, but whether it was that the empty baths were a bit dreary, or whether Specs was brooding over his measly sister, he didn't seem able to get up any speed at all. After a while we came out and dressed, and as it wasn't dinner-time yet we went for a walk along by the sea. The place was horribly deserted – only for Paddy the gardener, who was earthing up potatoes, and he's half-daft anyway – oh, and the Snooper, but it's always about, so we didn't count it. The Snooper is about three and belongs to Mr Olivers, the Art

Master. They live in a bungalow down near the shore, and since they had another baby in the autumn the Snooper seems to find a lot of time on its hands, and is always moping around to see if anything's happening.

We lay on the edge of the cliff and chewed grass and talked. The sea looked awfully nice, and we would have liked to have gone in, but it's out of bounds, and if anybody had seen us Specs would have been disqualified for the Swimming Sports, so it wasn't worth it. "I bet you I could swim better in there than in that old Dead Sea of a baths," said Specs, who was properly browned off. I let him moan away, thinking he would work it off, and I wasn't listening to him properly when suddenly he stopped, and I turned round to see why. He was staring down into the little bay below with a most extraordinary look on his face and his mouth hanging open, so I looked too. Then it was my turn to hang my mouth open.

Somebody was bathing there, not anybody from school. It was a girl. She was swimming backwards and forwards across the bay, to the rocks on one side and then to the rocks on the other, turning so fast at each side that her long yellow hair had hardly time to turn round after her before she had started off again. And could she swim? Specs's performance suddenly seemed very small beans. What you notice most about the champion swimmers at school is how hard they are trying, and how difficult it must be. But this girl was moving about twice as fast as anything I'd seen before, and she wasn't even trying. I never saw anything look so easy.

"Golly!" Specs whispered. And just then something

happened which is probably the most important thing in this story. A gust of wind took Specs's cap off his head and set it neatly on the water, just as the girl had turned round and was starting towards us again. She picked it up off the water, looked at it – and then she put it on and began to laugh, as pleased as Punch, and Specs and I laughed too. She heard us and looked up – and the next minute she was gone, straight down into the water like a stone, but as she went we saw something that made our eyes nearly fall out of our heads – it was the sun shining on a green and silver tail! "Golly!" said Specs again, and we sat quite still, looking at each other to make sure that if it was a dream at least there were two of us in it. We didn't say another word until the water broke again, and there she was, holding the cap in her hand and looking straight at us.

"I say," said Specs, "thanks awfully for my cap." "Nice cap!" the girl said. Specs said, "But I want it back, you know." "Do you?" asked the girl, and she looked very sad. "Please," said Specs. "No," the girl answered, holding on to the cap with both hands. I suppose she was treading water, so to speak, all the time, it certainly didn't seem to bother her. "Look here," argued Specs, "it's no use to you, and I shall get into a row if I lose it. You give it to me, and – I'll get you a better cap for yourself." "Will you?" she said, all smiles. "Of course I will," said Specs, thankful she was seeing sense, "anything you like." "What else'll you get me?" she asked. Specs had five sisters, but he wasn't much good at girls' things. "I tell you what," he suggested, "you tell me what you want, and I'll get it for you if" – he took a deep breath – "if you teach me to swim like you do."

4

"Well, I'll do my best," she said, "but I don't see how you could – not with legs." "I suppose it's easier with – for you," Specs said. She grinned. "You could always try," she said; "come on in and I'll show you." "I can't," Specs explained, feeling rather a fool, "we're not allowed in the sea." "Well, you can't swim on dry land," she laughed. Specs told her about the baths, making it sound as super as he could. She seemed quite excited. "Tell you what," Specs said, "come on up to the baths and teach me there." So in the end they struck a bargain – she was to come up to the baths, and Specs was to fetch her some clothes like she'd seen the smart bathing girls on the beaches wearing. I don't know where Specs thought he was going to get them, but he'd have promised anything for those swimming lessons. "Oh, and some of that red paint for my mouth and fingernails," she said, "and black for my eyebrows." Specs would have promised her the moon by this time. He saw himself shifting through the water at the Swimming Sports the way she did. "All right," he said; "we'll be here this afternoon – three o'clock sharp."

After dinner we counted up our money and legged it to the village shop – one of those shops that sell anything – and asked for eyebrow pencil and lipstick. The girl giggled a bit and asked what shade of lipstick. I never knew there were so many reds before. I fancied a kind of oxblood, but Specs said no, the brighter the better, and took some the colour of a fire engine, and some nail varnish to match. Just in the middle the shop-bell tinkled, and in came Mr Olivers, the art master, with the Snooper in tow. "Hallo, McCann," he said, "not gone home for half-term?" Specs explained about his sister.

"Measles?" said Olivers, "and you're going to manufacture some on yourself, are you?" He was grinning at the lipstick. The giggling girl let loose a cackle like a hen, and Specs wrung out a smile. "That's right, sir," he said, putting the stuff in his pocket and collecting the change. That's where Specs always scores – he lets the masters have their little jokes, so that they're never quite as funny as the masters think they're going to be. And we cleared out of the shop.

Eyebrow pencil and nail varnish and lipstick are much dearer than you'd think, for all the size they are, and we knew we couldn't rise to much in the way of clothes. "Why not try the Theatre Wardrobe at school?" I said. "There might be something there." Specs agreed, and we hoofed it back to school. It was a quarter to three, and Matron was setting off for the bus to the nearest picture-house. We told her we thought we'd put in a spot of dressing-up to while away the afternoon, and she felt sorry for us and gave us the wardrobe key. We chose the brightest thing we could – a Chinese coat Pooh Bah had worn when the Choral did the *Mikado*. Specs stuck it up his blazer, and we ran for the bay.

Halfway there Specs stopped suddenly. "I say, we are loony," he said; "how are we going to get her up to the baths? She can't walk, not with a – not the way she is." We felt so odd about it we didn't like to talk about it much, even to each other. "We could carry her," I said. "We could *not*," Specs answered, "she's as big as we are, and I'll bet she's slippery." Then I had a brain-wave. Paddy the gardener was making a celery trench. "The wheelbarrow," I said, "we could bring her along in that. Won't take a minute, and he'll never miss it."

Paddy was working at the far end of the trench, so we borrowed the wheelbarrow. He wouldn't think it queer of us, because he's a bit queer himself. Once clear of the garden we fairly rattled down the steep path to the bay.

She was putting in her time doing some fancy cuts, and she didn't notice us at first, so we stood and watched while Specs's eyes got too big for his spectacles. "See that?" he breathed. "Lovely, isn't it?" Then she saw us and came over. We gave her the stuff, and she seemed pleased, like a kid, and put the coat on at once. It was green with purple and gold dragons. She looked marvellous. "What about the paint?" she asked, and we handed it over. She put it on straight away, looking at herself in a pool and laughing. She overdid it a bit, it certainly was a very bright red. "What about the stuff for my nails?" she asked then. "You can do that later on," Specs said, "come on, hop in." She didn't seem too keen on the wheelbarrow, but we took it to the water's edge and with a good deal of heaving and shoving we got her over the edge and flop into the barrow. She was as helpless as a baby once she was out of the water. She wasn't a bit keen on leaving the sea either, but Specs gave her the nail varnish, and she sat in the wheelbarrow happily, painting her nails while we pushed and sweated and at last got the barrow up the path to the cliff top. We were mopping our brows and she was waving her hands about waiting for the stuff to dry when Specs suddenly froze. No wonder. Not fifty yards away Mr Olivers was sitting on a rock sketching. The Snooper was fooling around with an old golf club. Luckily, Mr Olivers was looking the other way. I was going to back the barrow down the cliff again, but Specs had a brain-wave. There was a huge pile of rotting seaweed lying at the top of the path – Paddy always brought it up after a high tide and left it there till he was ready to use it on the garden for manure – and Specs said "Mind your eye," and scooped a great armful of the stuff over the girl. She had the wit to keep still. The seaweed hid her pretty well, and we were just tucking in a sleeve of her coat when Olivers turned round. "Hallo," he called, "what are you up to?" "Bit of a loose end, sir," Specs explained, "just giving Paddy a hand." "The rash hasn't developed yet, has it?" asked Olivers, grinning. "I expect there'll be developments pretty soon, sir," said Specs, shoving away at the barrow like mad. The Snooper came careering towards us and poked at the seaweed with his golf stick. I tripped him up and Specs went ahead in showers of sand and little stones, and we didn't stop till we were at the baths. "Who was that you were talking to?" asked the girl, coming out of the seaweed. "He sounded nice. Pity you couldn't stop."

She seemed pleased with the baths when we got her in, though she asked why the water was such a funny colour. When Specs had rested a bit and felt better he went in too. The girl thought his swimming was funny at first, but Specs was so much in earnest he didn't mind her laughing. Then she started to show off, and it was some time before he got her down to business. I'll never forget the work they put in, once they started. "Like this?" Specs would say, slipping through the water like an eel. "More like this," she'd say, passing him without a ripple and coming back to meet him again, "if you lift your arm like this, and roll your shoulder ever so slightly." "Do it slowly," Specs would say, and she'd do it slowly. "Don't bother about breathing," she would say, "if you get there quick enough you can breathe afterwards." So Specs didn't bother. They were getting on like fun and I was sitting on the diving-board enjoying it, when there was a shadow in the doorway, and there stood Paddy the gardener. "So this is where youse are," he said. "Mr Olivers told me you'd taken the lend of the barrow." We waited to see what else he would say, but he took his pipe out of his mouth and blew a cloud of smoke before he let out, "You'll never swim anything near like her." We were too surprised to say anything. He puffed a while. "How do you know?" Specs asked. "Have you seen her swim before?" "Many's a time," said Paddy, "she be's playing herself when I'm fetching the wrack." "But why did you never tell anyone?" I asked. "Telling's no good to some folk," he grunted, "you get small thanks for it," and he stumped off. We heard him wheeling the barrow down the cinder path. We didn't say anything, but we were both thinking how many times we'd said Paddy was more than half daft.

After the swimming lesson had gone on a while, with Specs picking up the girl's tips very easily, they got hungry, and we decided to take her back. But how? We could get the barrow again, but what about Mr Olivers? I scouted around, and found he was still there, sketching away, and he said he thought the sunset would be worth waiting for, so I knew he was a fixture. We couldn't get the barrow down the path in the dark. There was nothing for it but to keep her in the baths overnight. She didn't like the idea, but we nipped up to the kitchen and fetched her down some provisions, and she said she'd stay.

All the same we didn't sleep too easy that night. It was just getting light next morning when we crept out into the garden and picked the lock of the toolhouse door for the barrow. The girl was feeling pretty dreary when we loaded her up. It was too risky to try and get her any breakfast from the kitchen, but we gave her a bar of chocolate and she cheered up. She sat in the barrow and did up her face while we wheeled her down the path. It was still too early for our breakfast, so after we had spilt her out on the rocks and she'd had a swim and felt much brisker she came back, and the three of us sat and talked, and ate more chocolate. She went over the instructions she'd given Specs. "Don't forget," she'd say, and Specs would say he wouldn't. Then we all shook hands and she slipped off into the water. I think she was sorry to go too.

Then we turned round to come up the path – and there was the Snooper. It was sitting throwing little pebbles into a pool. It looked as if it had been there for hours. "Nice," it said, and pointed to the water. I said it *was* a nice morning, wasn't it, and Specs bunged the last of the chocolate into its mouth and we went on.

So that was how Specs won the Swimming Championship. He didn't let anyone see just how good he was until the day of the Sports, and then – well, you'd almost have sworn he'd had a tail on him, the way he left the big chaps thrashing along behind him. He beat all records.

Next art class, Mr Olivers came over to where we

were working. "By the way, McCann," he said, "Tommy (that's the Snooper) says you swim nearly as well as the mermaid he saw you talking to down at the sea at half-term." Specs took the pencil he was sucking out of his mouth. "Wonderful the imagination kids have, sir," he said; "clever kids, I mean." "Yes, isn't it?" said Mr Olivers.

2

An Unnatural History Story

I spent last August at Tullybrannigan staying with Specs McCann and his family – you remember Specs who won the Swimming Sports? Specs has an awful clutch of sisters, mostly at the giggly age, so he and I thought we'd do a little natural history in the holidays, for an excuse to get away on our own; there was to be a prize offered at the Natural History Exhibition at school in September for the best of anything we had studied in the holidays. We're not keen on natural history really – I get hiccups when I'm bird-watching, and Specs falls over his feet, but the prizes were to be money, and we were both low in funds.

So whenever it wasn't pouring we took sandwiches and went off into the hills with notebooks and little tin boxes to put specimens in. It was rather a good act, and the girls were quite impressed. We weren't very energetic once we'd got away; often we lazed about and bathed in waterfalls and talked – at least Specs talked. He can talk about anything, and he says my ears are an inspiration to him.

I was lying in the heather in behind the shoulder of

Drinahilly one day, half listening to Specs talking, and half thinking that there was something to be said for natural history after all. The mountains were in a ring all round us: Drinahilly, Thomas's Mountain, Shan Slieve, up to Donard and round to the Millstone. There wasn't a house in sight, nothing but the hills and the heather – it might have been miles from anywhere. There wasn't a thing I could see, I thought to myself, that mightn't have been the same centuries and centuries ago. A bee went zooming past, and I wondered how many generations of his forbears had tasted the Donard heather. It was a frightening thought. "What's up?" asked Specs, "you do look queer." I told him what I was thinking. "There's nothing up here to show we're not right back slap into the Middle Ages," I said. He let out a cackle, and rolled over on his stomach to laugh better. "I suppose that's a medieval cigarette box you're sitting on," he hooted, and right enough I was sitting on some picnicker's litter. I threw the box at Specs and felt better. The sun was shining on his twentieth-century goggles, and time started to tick over again. We both laughed some more and unpacked the sandwiches.

A good while after lunch I said to Specs, "Let's walk over to the river there. I think there's a cave just where the waterfall starts." So we went across, but the cave wasn't up to much. Then the rain came on, and we hunkered down for a while. "Beastly draughty here," said Specs, "I bet there's more to this cave than meets the eye. This draught must have somewhere to come from." Well, we looked again, and right enough there was more to the cave, if you climbed over a big lump of granite and squeezed down the other side. Specs went

13

first. I wasn't too keen on following, for I had that awful feeling again, but Specs called, "Come along, can't you?" So I climbed over after him.

Specs was standing in a little chamber behind the huge granite block. It was just light enough to see. The roof was rock, jagged and uneven, and the walls were rock too. But somehow they were smooth – smooth as if they had been worn by something rubbing against them, year after year after year. "I wonder if anyone's ever lived here," said Specs, and I knew by his voice that he was as certain as I was that they had. "I say, what's that over there?" he said, and pointed. Lying on a ledge in one corner of the cave was something white and round – not round, either, it was oval – something like a melon or a small rugby ball. It was an enormous egg.

Specs whistled – a queer noise that ran right round the cave three times before it settled down. We touched the egg gingerly and there was layer upon layer of fine dust on it, dust that must have been gathering for years and years. But what made me jump was that – the egg was warm!

That was enough. Your two natural historians beat it for the daylight. The egg was too big and too fragile for us to squeeze it through the narrow entry – at least we told each other it was too big – and we decided to come up each day and keep an eye on it. So each day for four days we visited the cave and peered over, and on the fourth day there was a little crack across the monster egg, and we thought we could hear a faint scrambly noise inside, though we didn't listen too close.

The next day was one of those days when it just emptied from dawn to dusk, and we couldn't persuade

14

Mrs McCann that our natural history research could really be worth going up the hills for in that weather, so we spent hour after hour playing Up Jenkins and Rummy with the giggling sisters, and eating huge meals we weren't really hungry for.

The morning of the sixth day, however, was fine, and as soon as breakfast was over, we climbed up to the cave. It was a lovely morning, warm and shining, with the waterfalls thundering down. But as we got near the cave we thought we could hear something as well as the waterfalls, and we listened when we go to the opening. Yes, there was a noise. It was a cheerful scuffling noise – a scramble this way, then a little scuttering run the other way. Something with feet was making it. We couldn't speak for excitement, but over the granite block we went.

It *had* feet, four of them, and a little tail with a spike at the end. It had also scales, little wings, a large amiable head and eyes like a kitten. There wasn't any doubt about it – it was a baby dragon. It was playing by itself on the floor of the cave, chasing the shadows, pouncing on them, and then being surprised because there was nothing under its paws after all. It was so clumsy and lolloping we couldn't help laughing, partly from relief, and it sat up and looked at us with its head on one side. Specs went up to it slowly and scratched it behind its ear, and it began to purr and cocked its head to make the scratching feel better. "We'll take him out for a breath of air," said Specs, and putting it under his arm he scrambled out into the sun. Great man, Specs.

We could see the dragon better outside. He was just like the big ones, except for his baby eyes, and there was a sort of fluff over his scales, but this rubbed off as he got older. "How do you suppose he got here?" I asked. "Some kind of delayed action hatching," Specs said. "Now we know what used to live in that cave." "Hundreds and hundreds of years ago," I said, "and now it hatches out just in time for our Natural History Exhibition."

We stayed about an hour playing with the beast, and Specs taught him to beg for little tufts of grass and bilberry leaves; they seemed to be his favourite food, and then we sat down to think. "The thing is," said Specs, "I don't suppose we'll get the prize because nobody'll believe us." "We'll just have to take him with us," I said, "and make lots of notes in the meantime," and I pulled out my notebook and started to sketch the dragon pup, who was lying asleep on Specs's knees, worn out with exercise and excitement.

After that we came every day, rain or fine, and every day Egbert, the dragon pup, got bigger and stronger and more playful, and the fluff wore off his scales so that he glowed in the sun like polished brass. He could come out of the cave himself now, and often when we came up he would be trying to catch caterpillars, which he had discovered he liked better than grass or leaves. He was so clumsy on his feet that as often as not he would land on the caterpillars and squash them, and try to lick them off the ground, and get grit and soil in his mouth. So we used to catch them for him. He liked the smooth ones best, the hairy ones made his throat tickle. I gave him both kinds, because it took us much too long to gather smooth ones only, and if he chewed the hairy ones they went down all right.

One day we were all sitting outside the cave, and Specs and I were having our sandwiches. A piece of corned beef fell out of one, and before you could wink Egbert had snaffled it. Then he sat still in a kind of ecstasy, licking his lips round and round, and tried to bite a piece off the sandwich Specs was eating. Specs smacked and scolded him, and he was very sorry and went off and ate a lot of the hairy caterpillars he'd left from the day before. "It's going to be awkward if he gets carnivorous," Specs said. "Car—what?" "Meat-eating," said Specs, and right enough, when you thought about it, so it was. Egbert was beginning to grow ever so quickly now, and could roar quite well. He was also practising breathing fire, though steam was all he could manage.

We got hold of a big packing-case from a grocer and took it up the hill a few days before the end of the month (the girls were itching with curiosity about this). Egbert seemed quite fond of the case, and would go and sit down in it himself. We build him a little cave inside, with lumps of rock and clumps of heather. It looked very homely. Then for three whole days we collected caterpillars. I think we must have collected hundreds; big ones and little ones, green ones and black ones, striped ones and plain ones, ones with hair and bald ones, comic little stick caterpillars and huge striped monsters with eyes like searchlights. Egbert didn't help, he just sat in his box and looked a bit disgusted. At last the day came. The McCanns were going home on an early train, but Specs and I asked if we could stay till the late one, for one last walk in the hills, and I think Mrs McCann was quite glad. So after we'd seen them off – you'd have thought those girls were going to America – we climbed the hill for the last time. Egbert was sulky because we were late, and he'd caught a young rabbit and made his dinner off it. There wasn't much of it left. We bundled him into the packing-case, and he sat over in the corner sulking and taking no notice of the swarms of caterpillars we had provided.

He was fairly quiet in the train, except when he started to breathe steam and an old countrywoman in the carriage complained of the way the railway company used good coal to heat up the train in the summer. I stowed the box in an old shed near the tennis courts. Nobody was back at school yet, except matron and the maids, and they were busy all the time. I was worried about Egbert though. Whether it was the feed of rabbit or the sulks, he wouldn't eat a single caterpillar. However, the exhibition was the second day of term, so we hadn't long to wait.

When Specs and I came staggering into the lab with the closed box there was a lot of comic inquiry. All sorts of collections were laid out – I suppose lots of people were a bit low in funds after the holidays. Hawkins had a family of young mice and a hedgehog, and there were butterflies, flowers, rocks, shells, and lots of other things. We didn't open our box until the last moment, just when the biology master told us to clear out because he was going for the judges, and even then we were the last out. "Now, Egbert," we whispered, "you're going to be a sensation. Do your stuff." Egbert was sitting very quietly, but there was a wicked look in his eye – a carnivorous look, you might say.

We all hung about waiting for the judges to come across from school. They took what seemed like all afternoon to do it. Specs got impatient. "Look here," he said, "I'm going to nip in by the back, just to see if he's all right," and he was off like a shot.

Just as the judges were at the front door Specs shot round from the back, and his face was as white as a sheet. "He's gone!" he gasped, pulling me away from the others. "He's hopped it, skedaddled, whatever you like. His cord was bitten through. The big window was open, he's gone that way, through the garden. There's gratitude for you." We were so sick about it we didn't say much more. As well as losing the money we'd seem such fools. Luckily Specs had had the sense to bring away our book of notes and drawings.

For the sake of appearance we hung around, and at last the biology master and the judges came out and stood in the doorway. After the usual humming and hawing the chief judge began to speak. I wasn't listening properly, but the first thing I heard was that the prize was awarded to McCann and Curtis "for their outstanding collection of caterpillars". "These young exhibitors," said the judge, "conceived the clever notion of presenting the caterpillars in an extremely realistic copy of their natural habitat. Their collection includes many rare varieties, among them the Northern Egger and the Hawk Moth. I am only sorry they have not listed the collection, but doubtless they will make amends for this. It must have taken endless patience and great powers of observation to muster it, and imagination to give it such a setting."

"You're telling me," sighed Specs who was the first to recover.

It was bad luck on Hawkins though; his family of mice had disappeared, though the hedgehog was still there. I suppose hedgehogs are even worse than hairy caterpillars, but I was glad Egbert had a square meal before he left.

3

Specs by Moonlight

I couldn't get Specs woken that morning. I'd done my best, but he must have been in the middle of a dream because even when I pulled the pillow out from under his head and bawled down his ear that the second bell had gone he just smiled in a silly sort of way, said "Yes dear," with his eyes tight shut, and went on snoring. So I pulled the clothes right off him, and went down by myself.

There were two letters on his plate. I guessed that one was the *Meccano* catalogue he had sent for, but I couldn't help wondering who the other was from. It wasn't his mother's writing, though it was her turn to write. Besides, it was a long pale mauve envelope, and the address was written in very fancy handwriting in green ink. The masters were late coming in for breakfast, and Specs made it just before the door closed, buttoning and hitching and tying for all he could go. "You might have woken me," he grunted, and I was just going to tell him all about it when he spotted the letters. He made a grab for the mauve one and stuffed it into his trouser pocket without a word, and then spread the Meccano

21

catalogue out on top of the marmalade and began to eat his porridge. But I thought he turned a funny colour, and he took a look down at his pocket now and again, as if he thought the mauve envelope would put its head out and snap at him.

I was itching with curiosity by this time, but I just had to itch until break. By that time the coolness about not waking him had died out. "Come on down to the cinder track with me," Specs said, "and look as if you were talking while I read this letter." Even then, he didn't open it until he was sure none of the other chaps were watching. "Why all this mystery business?" I asked. "Who in the world is it from?" "From Puppy," said Specs in a disgusted sort of voice, and he waved the sheet of notepaper in my face. "Smell!"

Right enough it smelt like a classy chemist's shop. "It's a good thing there's a strong wind," Specs said, looking over his shoulder to make sure no one was coming. "It's better than anything they do in the lab. She always uses scented notepaper. Phew! What a girl!"

Puppy is one of Specs's sisters. He's got five of them, and she is the youngest. It's an awful name, isn't it? They've all got awful names like that, that they use in the family – hangovers from the nursery. I nearly died the first time I was staying with them and I heard them call Specs – no, it just wouldn't be fair to tell you what they call him at home, but it gives me the shudders every time I hear it. Anyhow, this Puppy is the youngest of them. The others are more or less grown up, and she's been spoiled. They used to try to spoil Specs, but they gave that up as a bad job and concentrated on Puppy. So she really is rather awful.

Specs groaned when he'd read the letter. "Just listen to this," he said, "I'm to go to see a Fairy Play – you'll have to come too," and he waved two tickets at me. "Better hold them in the breeze to get the smell off them," he went on, "we can burn the letter, but if we have to go to this Fairy Play we must hang on to the tickets."

It seemed that Puppy was at a dancing class, and they were giving a children's matinee in Belfast, in aid of some charity or other, and neither Specs's father or mother, nor any of the other sisters could get up to Belfast that afternoon. That was why Specs had to go. Puppy was going to be heartbroken if none of them were there to see her performance, so Specs was to represent the family. Mrs McCann had written to the headmaster (that's my father) explaining about it all and asking for leave. There were two tickets so that he could bring a friend, so of course the friend had to be me – really, the things I do for Specs!

It turned out to be the afternoon of one of the house-matches, when everybody else was going up to the rugger field. It was a gorgeous day too, just the sort of day we could have spent shouting ourselves hoarse on the touchline, and here we were, off to a children's Fairy Play. We felt very browned off when we reached the theatre. Puppy was waiting for us, just inside. She's a thin little girl with stringy pigtails and glasses, and a sharp sort of nose. "Oh, there you are, darling –" she called out, using that awful name for Specs that I must remember not to tell you, and she put her arms round his neck and hugged him. "Isn't it thrilling, and wasn't it clever of me to get you off school for a treat like this?"

She didn't hug me, because I saw it coming and shook hands with her instead. "Hadn't you better get along and change?" Specs said, "you haven't much time." "I'm not on till the second act," Puppy squealed, "I just wanted to be sure you were here. It would have been so dreadful if there'd been nobody here from the family to see me." "What are you supposed to be?" Specs growled. "Oh, didn't I tell you?" she fluttered. "I'm a moonbeam – all our class are moonbeams. We come stealing into the wood at night." "It would be funny if you came in the daytime," Specs grunted, but she was in a kind of silver daze about the whole business. "We come floating in," she said, "ever so gently while the orchestra plays ever so softly, and we drift around among the trees ever so prettily – oh, it's lovely, you'll love it, I know you'll love it. Now I really must go – you'll be all right, won't you, you can find your seats, can't you?" "If the moonbeams shine bright enough we'll be there by the second act," said Specs, sounding terribly fed up, but she laughed and called him by that dreadful name, and said, "You are awful," and then before he could dodge she kissed him, gave him a bag of toffees and hopped it quick.

"Think of it," said Specs, after we had fallen over a lot of people's feet and had found our own seats, "I might have been at the match, telling our chaps what to do, and here I am, sitting at a Fairy Play, a moonbeam's brother." Then he put a couple of the moonbeam's toffees into his mouth and pushed the bag over to me, and we had just started to chew when the curtain went up.

The first act was pretty terrible. There were some great whacking trees in the background and a hedge business in front of them, and in front of that, in the middle of the stage, a fountain affair. A girl was sitting crying into the fountain, but after a bit she cheered up enough to sing a song explaining that she was the youngest princess and that her sisters, who had all been smashers, had gone and got themselves princes for husbands, and she was left sitting on the shelf, or rather on the edge of the fountain. After that she sat down to cry again. Then all sorts of flower-fairies from the palace garden came in and danced, girls in pink frocks for roses and yellow frocks for sunflowers, and that kind of idea. There was one of the sweetpeas, one with red hair, who danced a bit all by herself, rather well, I thought, but when I whispered something about her to Specs he gave me a disgusted look and stuck another toffee into his mouth. He was determined to be gloomy about the whole affair, and sat heaving great gusty sighs. By the time the curtain went down at the end of the act he really was beginning to be rather a nuisance and people were starting to notice him. He made matters worse by turning to me and saying in a loud voice, "Isn't it awful? Did you ever see anything so wet?" and I could fairly feel the people on each side of us bristle. You see, we were sitting in the middle of all the fond relations, and for all we knew the doleful princess's mother might have been in front of us, and the red-haired sweetpea's grannie in the row behind. Altogether we were getting very unpopular, and I spent the interval trying to make Specs understand.

When the curtain went up again it was the same scene, only in moonlight. "This is it," said Specs in a hollow voice, "Operation Moonbeam." And right enough from each side of the stage came the moonbeams, all sizes and shapes, fat ones, skinny ones, big ones, little ones. I spent a long time trying to pick out Puppy. I thought I'd know her by the glasses and pigtails, but none of the moonbeams were wearing either pigtails or glasses. At last I saw one standing at the side of the fountain on the tip of her toe, fixing the audience with a particular fetching simper, and I discovered it was Puppy without her glasses, and with her hair hanging round her loose.

Specs must have seen her too. He gave a kind of disgusted groan, as if he couldn't stand it any longer, and got to his feet. Naturally I followed. We fell across people's knees until we reached the aisle. "Where are you going?" I whispered. "Out of this," he said grimly. Well, it wasn't as easy as it sounded. We must have taken the wrong turning because we found ourselves in a corridor that led into another corridor that led up a few steps, and then into another corridor again. "I believe we're round the back of the stage," I said; "what'll they say if they find us here?" "They're all much too busy to find us," he grunted. "Anyway, I'm a moonbeam's brother."

Certainly there wasn't anyone about. We wandered along until we found a door that was open, and then we went in. It was a big room, and at one end was a whacking great cupboard lying open, with all sorts of things inside – crowns, and suits of armour, statues, a birdcage, a harp, a cradle, some plaster fish. "Look," said Specs suddenly and pulled out a horse's head – not just the head, but the head was the only part of the horse that was solid. The rest was made of hairy cloth, cloth body, cloth legs, with a really handsome tail. It was one of those stage horses that you see in circuses, with room for a couple of men inside it. "I've always wanted to know what these were like," Specs said, and right enough, so had I. There was a zip business running along the horse's tummy. "That's where you get in," he said, and without waiting, he did. He got into the skin and put his legs down the front legs of the horse and the head over his own head. "Hop in behind," he said, and – well, what would you have done? I hopped in and when I had fixed my feet into the hind hoofs of the horse I found there was a wizard piece of rope for making the tail work, so I practised on that while Specs zipped us up. "Might have been made for us," he said, "let's go places." Of course we fell over when we tried to move, and it took us a bit of time getting disentangled and learning how to work together. It was rather like a three-legged race in the dark. It wasn't so bad for Specs – there were peep-holes in the head that he could see through – but it was all I could do to follow his step. After I got the hang of it we went round the room a couple of times, and got so expert that we worked up to a smart trot. Then all of a sudden I felt that the floor under my feet wasn't the wooden floor of the room any more, but the concrete floor of the corridor. "Look out, Specs," I called, yanking at him, "we're out of the room." Specs didn't pay the slightest attention. All he did was to quicken up into a smart canter. I knew we wouldn't get far without being spotted, but what could I do? Wait till you're the back end of a determined horse, and you'll see what I mean. I couldn't see where we were, but I could hear the music from the stage getting nearer and nearer, dreamy moonlight sort of music. Specs heard it too and broke into a kind of Vienna waltz without telling me, and it was a while before I got my end waltzing to match.

I don't know how we got so far without being stopped. Of course most of the dancers were on the stage, and those that weren't had crowded into the wings to watch. The music was quite loud now. Suddenly Specs said, "Come on – next stop the moon!" and he charged forward. Through the lines of stitching on my skin the pale blue moonlight was coming in. We were on the stage!

I shall always be sorry I couldn't see what happened next. I was just ploughing about in the half dark at my end, hanging on to Specs for dear life and trying to follow his footwork. He says himself it was a superb performance, and I take his word for it. I know he went in like a charger entering the lists. The moonbeams shrieked and stopped short in their dance. They stood there gaping while Specs bore down on them, and then they scattered, squealing, in all directions. A few of them got to the wings, but most of them ran from side to side with Specs chasing them. He pranced and pounced and rounded up the ones who were trying to escape and sent them scuttering down towards the footlights. One of them tried to climb a tree, but of course the whole thing just came down on top of her. Another – Specs says it was the red-haired sweetpea – fell into the fountain and lay there kicking madly while Specs snapped at her feet. The orchestra whined away for a few bars and then stopped altogether, from pure astonishment. And then there came a great wave of sound from across the footlights. The audience were laughing! Laughing? I should say they were! As Specs said they hadn't had the ghost of a laugh since the show started, and now they were making up for lost time.

Of course the laughter went to Specs's head completely. He did some fancy footwork that made them laugh even louder – it isn't often you see the front end of a horse doing the splits – but when he went and took a great drink out of the fountain and wiped his mouth with his forefoot, they began to stamp and clap as well. And, though I say it myself, there was some pretty masterly tail-work going on all the time. Only there isn't so much scope at the back end, is there?

It was just then, when the applause was at its peak, that Specs, with what he calls his perfect sense of timing, beat it for the wings. And because our exit was so unexpected, we got through without being stopped. Most of the grown-ups who were running the show were busy picking up and straightening the moonbeams, and the stage hands weren't quite sure if we were part of the act or not. So we got along to the room again, and nipped out of the skin and into the corridor just as an angry lady zoomed round the corner. She asked what we were doing there, and Specs said he was worried about his little sister who was one of the moonbeams, so we got past her all right, and in the middle of the hubbub, found our way out into the street. By more good luck we got a bus which landed us up at school for the last fifteen minutes of the match – that was good going!

Specs never mentioned the affair after that. He's funny sometimes. But I went to stay with the McCanns this holidays, and I knew the subject would come up some time or other. The sisters were all at home – Bubbles and Birdie and Toots and Fiddles and Puppy. Ghastly names, aren't they, but nothing to what they call Specs. Anyhow, the first evening when we were all sitting round at tea I was feeling pretty nervous. Mrs McCann was busy behind the teapot. She looked across at me, and said, "You went to see Puppy in the Fairy Play, didn't you?" I said yes, and it had been very kind of her to send me a ticket. I could feel Puppy's eyes on me. It seemed odd that nobody said anything about the pantomime horse that had gatecrashed the show. It looked as if Puppy hadn't told them. I wondered why. Was it because she guessed?

"It was nice of you to go," said Mrs McCann. "Of course they went," said Puppy. Then she looked over at Specs and said, "You wouldn't look a gift horse in the mouth, would you?" From the way she said it, I knew she knew. Specs didn't say anything, he just pretended his mouth was too full. "Would you?" said Puppy again, leaning across the table at him, "would you, Dimple?"

That's torn it – I've told you. Oh, how awful! Look, don't say a word about it to Specs, will you? He'd slay me! Dimple! I told you it was a perfectly ghastly name, didn't I, and was I right?

4

Specs and that Awful Dog

We were lying comfortably in the shade watching the cricket match between the masters and the parents when Matron came clucking along, waving her camera at us. "Now," she twittered, "this will make a nice informal little group. Don't get up, just turn this way, and I'll get you all in."

It was too hot really to bother turning round; besides, the match had got to rather a tricky stage, with Specs's father, Dr McCann, batting, and only another ten minutes to win; however we rolled around to oblige Matron. Her big ginger cat, that follows her about, came and sat all over us and got shoved off. Matron said, "Now, boys, be kind to Mr Tomkins; he wants his photo taken just as much as you do." We didn't, but nobody liked to point this out, and we all put on suitable smirks, or looked fierce, according to which way a camera affected us. "Put your hair out of your eyes, McCann," Matron said, "you should have gone to the barber a fortnight ago." Specs changed his smirk for a scowl – he and Matron are always waging war about his hair, he favours the poetic, and she likes the convict cut. "Russel, you're very flushed

– you aren't running a temperature, are you?" she asked, and Tusky Russel got brighter red and said no, he wasn't. I cleared my throat in a meaning way and Matron promised me a gargle. Then she took her snap. After that was over we settled down again to watch the match. Mr Tomkins was too lazy to move on with Matron; he sat down beside us, and we ate oranges and amused ourselves trying to score a direct hit on him with the pips. Matron's soppy about that cat. You should hear the way she talks to him when she thinks no one's listening! They say when she's got no one in the san she takes his temperature night and morning, to keep herself in practice. The cat didn't pay any attention to the orange pips – he just twitched an ear, or hit out lazily with the nearest paw. I think he was rather glad to be having a rest from Matron too.

Meanwhile Specs's father had produced another run – he's one of these cautious prodders who stay in for hours without doing very much. Then he sent up an easy catch, and Mr Wilde, the French master, dropped it, so we roused up enough to produce an ironic cheer. This lucky escape went to Dr McCann's head, and when Mr Wilde sent him down a leg ball he hooked it for four, slap into the middle of us and Matron's cat. The cat wasn't hit, but he must have felt the draught, for he let a howl out of him, and Matron came twittering up to treat him for shock. Meanwhile the ball went and lost itself in the long grass beneath the hedge, and we had to get up and hunt for it.

It was while the game was hung up like this, and the players were yelling at us to hurry up with the ball, that the awful dog made his first appearance. It came bounding on to the pitch from nowhere at all, and stood just behind Dr McCann. He turned round and shouted at it, and it just stood and waved its great bushy tail amiably, and knocked the bails off. The umpire came bustling up to put them on again and Dr McCann shook his bat at the dog who proceeded to dig a hole in the middle of the precious pitch. Everybody shouted at it, and just because we felt sorry for it Specs and I went and brought it out of harm's way, and it sat very happily and heavily on us for the rest of the match, and licked our faces. It was one of those large hairy dogs, with a tail like a banner, and a wet pink tongue that was always hanging out. It had big soft eyes and an inquiring nose, and a very trusting expression, as if it was sure everybody would be delighted to see it at any time. It must have been hungry too, for it wolfed some scraps of biscuit Specs found in his pocket.

It disappeared again just as suddenly after the match. Specs had saved up his bun from supper, and he went out into the grounds to look for it, thinking it might still be hungry, but there wasn't a sign of it. All through the term, though, it kept appearing and disappearing. It walked in on one of my mother's tea parties – my father's the headmaster – and sent a whole cakestand of cakes on to the floor. It waited till Mr Wilde, who's keen on birds, had climbed the big chestnut tree to look into the woodpigeon's nest, and then it parked itself underneath the tree and growled very fiercely every time Mr Wilde tried to get down. Specs came in the end and led it away, and it went off with him peaceably, wagging its great tail and grinning fit to bust. As often as we could we gave it food, and it was always hungry. None of us knew where its home was, or if it had a home. It had a most affectionate disposition – too affectionate really. It pranced into the linen room one afternoon while Matron was counting piles of sheets and pillowcases and towels, and after it had climbed over most of them with its muddy paws it landed up in Matron's lap, gazing at her with devotion. You should have seen her face – and her white coat. After that we made a bed for him in the old stable at the end of the cinder track, and we took him out for walks whenever we could, and brought him all the food we managed to scrounge. I must say he was an awfully hungry dog, but he was always very pleased to see us and very grateful for everything we did.

Matron got those photos developed and brought them into the dorm one night to show us. "Just look," Specs said, without thinking, "who's the minor prophet in the back row?" And then of course he realized it was himself – I told you his hair was long. "I don't really look like that," he said. "Of course you do," said Matron, "I told you it was a shocking length. Truth will out – the camera cannot lie, you know." So after that there was nothing he could do but go and have it cut, and he came back nearly bald.

Next day he came out in a lovely speckly rash. He says it was shock and exposure after his haircut, but I think myself it was gooseberries – we'd visited the bushes the evening before. The doctor didn't know what it was, but he packed Specs off to the san until something decided to develop. So I went down to the old stable and fed that awful dog myself and he was so happy and pleased about things that he nearly knocked me down. But he looked very sadly at me with his big wet eyes when I told him about Specs.

Next day I was out in a rash as well (which proved it must have been the gooseberries) so I was packed off to the san, too. Specs wasn't a bit pleased to see me. "Who d'you think's going to look after that awful dog, and see he gets his food if we're both here?" he growled, "what did you want to go and get spotty for?" I pointed out that the spots had been his idea, but I was feeling too queer to argue. Next day, when my head was better, I began to think about that poor awful dog hanging about the stable waiting for his food, and the more I thought the more it got on my mind. Specs was much perkier that day, and he thought up a scheme. There was an iron fire escape from the window of the san, and while Matron was at breakfast he sneaked down and fetched the dog back with him. We fed it with what we'd saved off our breakfast trays, and it ate the lot, and tried to lick the spots off our faces. We got it shoved out of the window just before Matron came back. "Now it knows where we are, it should be all right," Specs said, "if it has any sense it'll report here for rations."

That awful dog had plenty of that kind of sense, and three or four times a day for the next few days it would arrive at the window, by way of the fire escape, and collect whatever food he managed to keep for it. Matron was awfully bucked to see we had found our appetites again – such a good sign, she said. Then one warm afternoon Matron came in and said the ward felt stuffy, and she flung open all the windows, and in pranced that awful dog and climbed up on to Specs's bed and lay on his chest, wagging its huge tail amiably at the Matron.

This was the end. Matron was lepping mad. That awful dog again, she said, were we never going to see

35

the last of him, look at the marks on the bedspread, dogs in a sickroom, very unhealthy, whose dog was he anyhow, people had no right to let a dog run loose like that, if he hadn't a proper home then it was time one was found for him, she would find one, she would see about it. All this she said, and more, and that awful dog got down off Specs's chest and went over to Matron and sat up in front of her and begged. Now, you know, Matron is an awful old cluck, but she has a very kind heart, and I didn't think she'd be able to resist the dog's appeal to her better nature, especially with his eyes fixed on her so trustingly, and his tongue hanging out so far. But she did, and led him off downstairs, saying the same things over again, all the way down.

Next day that awful dog didn't turn up at the window, and when we asked Matron about him she said that a home had been found for him, and that was all we could get out of her. Specs was furious and he tried to have a relapse, just to spite her, but his temperature had come down and wouldn't go up again, and he couldn't go off his food because he was so hungry after keeping most of his meals to feed the dog for the last day or two. So he decided to get better instead, and see if he couldn't find out for himself where the dog was. And by the end of the week both our rashes had gone, and we were allowed to go back to school again.

But there wasn't a trace of the dog. We visited the stable quite often, but it never turned up, and although we left food at the top of the fire escape he never came to eat it. But some funny things happened, which made Specs suspicious. I'll say this about Specs, he is good at putting two and two together, even if it doesn't always make four. One day he had to take a message to Matron after school – she lives in a little cottage at the front of the long drive when she's not sleeping at the san – and when he came back he was simply goggling. Matron's doorstep, he said, was black with dog's paw-marks. "So what?" I asked, rather scornfully. "The dogs round about are always chasing Mr Tomkins, and I expect one of them has been sitting at the front door waiting for him to come out." "They were very *big* paw-marks," Specs said, thoughtfully. Matron was late for tea that night – she sits at our table – and when she did come she looked very blown about and her shoes were muddy, not a bit like Matron. She'd been for a walk, we heard her tell Mr Olivers, a walk up into the country. Specs's eyes lit up like searchlights, and he told Matron did she know she'd torn her stocking? Matron just said no, had she, and went on talking to Mr Olivers, but she didn't seem a bit pleased.

Next day we were in surgery getting my hand done up – I'd squashed my finger at carpentry – and Specs, who'd come along with me, happened to say to Matron that he thought Mr Tomkins was getting rather thin. "He hasn't been ill, has he?" he asked. Matron said no, Mr Tomkins was quite all right, he might be a bit thinner but that wouldn't do him any harm, he'd always been rather fat. And Specs turned a careful eye on me, and winked. We knew now that we'd guessed right, and that that awful dog had wangled its way round Matron and made a home for itself in her cottage, and that she was too ashamed to let any of us know. I hadn't been wrong when I'd bargained on its wet eyes and Matron's soft heart. I must say Matron kept her secret very well. Her cottage was a tiny one, and that awful dog must have taken up a lot of room in it. And she must have walked it for miles. It was no wonder Mr Tomkins looked less pleased with himself.

Our Pets' Club was holding its Annual Meeting at the end of term. We always have an exhibition and a special tea, you know the kind of affair. Matron's the President, and she and Mr Tomkins always preside over the tea. Well, everybody came, Tusky with his pigeons, Ellis with his guinea-pigs, the little Alexander with a bowl of goldfish, White and his hedgehog, and all the others. Specs and I were there, we were still members although we hadn't any pets that term – no official pets, only that awful dog, and of course we'd lost it. It was a lovely tea, and Matron was in great form, only Mr Tomkins didn't appear. We asked why, and she said she was sorry but he'd got rather stupidly shy lately, and so she'd left him at home. After tea we went out into the garden to have a photo taken. Seeing he had no pet to hold, Specs took the photo – Matron in the middle, and all the boys, guinea-pigs, budgies, pigeons, goldfish, etc, grouped around. He said he'd have the film developed for Matron – and he had a message to the chemist anyway, so it wouldn't be any trouble.

A couple of days afterwards he came in to tea waving the packet of prints. He'd called for them, he said, on the way up. Matron opened them. "Now let's see if it does us and our little friends justice," she twittered, and then "Oh!" and she stopped and gaped at the photo in her hand, and her mouth just hung open. Then she turned to Specs. "McCann," she said, "I think surely there must have been some mistake." "Mistake, Matron?" Specs said, looking mildly surprised behind his goggles. "Oh no, Matron. The camera cannot lie. Truth will out."

Then we all made a grab for the photo. It was a very good photo really, Tusky, the hedgehog, little Alexander, the budgies, the goldfish, Ellis and the guinea-pigs, all as clear as possible and most lifelike. It was good of Matron too. She was sitting in the middle of the group, in her nice white coat, with a pleased smile, and on her lap – on her lap, with an even more pleased smile and his tongue hanging so far out it didn't seem safe, sat that awful dog.

I don't really understand the whole business myself. I asked Specs but he just shut up and wouldn't talk, he's like that sometimes. I don't know if he faked the negative, or if it was just another of those queer things that happen to him. But it finished Matron's little game. That awful dog has the run of the school now, and he follows her everywhere, very fat and meek, and Specs and I have taken to making friends with Mr Tomkins on the sly, because he's rather on our conscience.

5

Specs and the White Rabbit

Art used to be rather a wet sort of subject at school, but since Mr Olivers started this wheeze about abstract art and significant form his shares have gone up no end. It isn't surprising, when you think of it. Instead of having to copy four daffodils in a jampot, or a dictionary with an inkpot and a tennis ball on it, or designing a Christmas card, we mess about painting abstracts, and a good time is had by all.

Perhaps you don't know about abstracts. I don't know an awful lot about them myself, but I have got the hang of the general idea. Instead of painting things the way they look, you paint shapes which suggest the idea of things, but aren't really pictures of them at all. That sounds odd, I know, but it isn't nearly as odd as some of our pictures. Mr Olivers explained all about it one day, and told us to go ahead. Well, everybody sat about scribbling a little and then rubbing it out, or mixing away at their paints and then looking up at the ceiling and heaving great sighs, but nobody got on with it. Mr Olivers saw how uninspired we were. "Come on, you fellows," he said, "let's see you all expressing yourselves

– you're not afraid of form and colour, are you? We want masses of colour, strong blues, mysterious crimsons, greens that shout – a riot!" Tusky Russel, who had so far produced one pale pink tadpole in the middle of his page put another pale pink tadpole beside it, but apart from this everybody looked blanker than ever. Meanwhile, Mr Olivers went out of the room to fetch a book he wanted to show us, and we all relaxed and began to wish we were back where we'd been before all this started, painting four daffodils in a jampot.

Then Specs got suddenly fed up – at least that's what I say, but he says he felt a sudden wave of inspiration. "All right," he said, "if it's colour he wants, here's how." And he sloshed a great wash of bright staring orange right across his page, and before it had dried he put a purple crab sitting on the top of it, only it wasn't really a crab because it was wearing a bowler hat, not a bowler hat actually, because it had wings, not real wings, but – oh well, that's enough to give you an idea of what the picture was like. And just as he was finishing by filling up the spare spaces with great blue raspberries, Mr Olivers came in again. The rest of the class was sitting just where he'd left them, in a kind of hopeless fog, but Specs was working away like anything, at the last of his raspberries. Mr Olivers came over and stood at his elbow, watching him. "Well, McCann," he said, as Specs took breath to see if he could squeeze another raspberry in anywhere, "well, McCann, *you've* got the idea all right." Specs was too surprised to say anything. "Yes – yes, indeed," Mr Olivers went on, "that's a very subtle purple – and such a *brave* green. Oh, I like that" – he leant forward and poked his finger at the thing that was

41

like a bowler hat – "I like the shape of that – it's very significant."

After that the rest of us soon got the idea of what was wanted, and we slapped away happily at scarlets and blues and greens, and produced all kinds of very significant shapes, and Mr Olivers was frightfully braced. But because Specs had been the first to see the light he was always rather the white-headed boy. And that was why, when the Olivers' kid – the Snooper, if you remember the Snooper – was having his birthday party, Mr Olivers asked Specs to come and help with the games – and of course seeing he was asking Specs I was asked as well. We weren't madly keen on the idea, actually, but it meant getting off some prep and having a jolly good tea. Besides, Mr Olivers said there was to be a conjuror.

Specs and I got dickied up early that afternoon and arrived at the Olivers' bungalow a little before time, to see if there was anything we could do. Mrs Olivers gave us a lot of balloons to blow up. We'd had an awful hurry to get there, and these were the tough obstinate little balloons that are so hard to get started. First of all we puffed and panted without making any impression on them, but at last we got our wind back. Even then it wasn't too easy. I had the round balloons, and they blew up all right until they were the size of a grapefruit and then just burst in my face. Specs had the long ones, and they blew up into all sorts of funny shapes – a bulb at the tip and then a long thin neck, or a diseased banana, you know the way they go. I had just burst my seventh balloon, and Specs was killing himself laughing at the silly shape of the one he was blowing when Mr Olivers came in to see how we were getting along. He didn't seem too pleased. "Get a move on," he said, "they'll be here any time now, and look how few you've got ready." "But look at this one, sir," said Specs, holding up his latest effort. It was like – well, it really was a frightfully silly shape, but Mr Olivers eyed it thoughtfully and stroked the new little beard he is so proud of. "Yes, McCann," he said, "it is interesting." "Significant, sir?" asked Specs, and Mr Olivers agreed it was very significant.

Just then the front door bell began to ring, and there wasn't much peace in the house after that. I don't really know if you've had any experience of kids' parties. Certainly the Snooper's little friends were a very muscular set. There was one small girl in a frilly white dress who'd have been a gift in the scrum. We wore them down a little playing all sorts of games, and then paused for breath and had another whack at it. Then Mrs Olivers came in to say that tea was ready, and they all let go of us at once and beat it for the dining-room, and in ten seconds the place was quiet, except for the sound of chewing and swallowing. Mrs Olivers had said she'd give us our tea in the drawing-room, and right enough in she came with a tray. I don't know when I've been so hungry – you should try "Musical Bumps" for getting up an appetite.

We were sitting there relaxing and chewing when the door opened and a little man in a dark suit came in, and Mrs Olivers after him. "This is Mr Edwardo," she said, "he's going to entertain the children after tea." The little man had a black suitcase with him, and he left it down in a corner of the room and went off with Mrs Olivers to have tea. "And to meet the kiddies," he said, rubbing his pale long hands together very quickly, and smiling, "I always like to get to know my little friends." We sat and ate, and looked at our bruises, and thought he could have his little friends to himself. We ate everything that was on that tray, and by the time we had finished we couldn't stir. At least I couldn't but Specs can always stir if he's interested enough, and that conjuror's black suitcase drew him like a magnet. "I wouldn't half like to see what's inside," he said. "You'd much better not touch it," I warned him, "it'll be locked anyway." But it was no use talking to him. He picked the suitcase up and fingered the clasps lovingly, and one of them flew open. "There!" he said, "What did I tell you?" "It was me that was telling you," I said, "you leave that case alone."

But there's no use talking to Specs sometimes. And once he'd got the case open I just had to come and look as well. It was all fitted up like a doctor's case inside. Little boxes, lots and lots of them, and cylinders with screw tops, a round shining silver ball that was cold when you felt it, a couple of bright silk handkerchiefs, and, fitted into a groove at the side, a long tapering wand. Specs pulled this wand out to have a look at it. There was a little bulb at the point, and it lit up when you pressed a knob on the handle. This pleased Specs no end. He started fooling about with the thing, waving it in the air, and shouting, "Abracadabra! Cadabra Cadoo! The next living creature to come through that door I will transform and transfigure!" I told him for goodness sake to shut up, and just at that moment the door opened and Mr Olivers came in. "I say, have you chaps got enough to eat in here?" he asked, and then – then – quite suddenly – he wasn't there! He – he faded out. There wasn't anybody there, but sitting on the carpet where he had been a moment ago – there was a large solemn white rabbit!

I looked at Specs and he looked at me, and we both looked at the rabbit. It wasn't very interested in us, but just sat there, twitching its soft nose and scratching one ear with one hind paw. Then it sniffed at the carpet, took a lollop forwards and sat down again to scratch the other ear.

Now this was awful – you can see how awful it was! There was Mr Olivers turned into a white rabbit in his own drawing-room. The noise from the dining-room had started up again, the children had nearly finished feeding, and they would soon be coming back – not only the children, but the conjuror and Mrs Olivers. It was an absolutely super white rabbit but – well, she wouldn't like it – I mean, who would? "Can't you turn him back?" I said to Specs, but he just shook his head; his face was the colour of a beetroot. And the white rabbit sat there blinking at us and twitching its nose.

I will say this much for Specs, he's good at deciding what to do in a jam – after all he's got into so many jams he's had plenty of practice. He slid the wand into its place in the suitcase and closed the lid. "The thing to do," he said, "is to get him out into the garden."

Now I saw the sense of this myself. A white rabbit in the drawing-room does take a good deal of explaining, and once it was outside there was always the hope that it would hop off and lose itself among the bushes. "Look," said Specs, going close to the rabbit, "look – sir – this is a bit awkward. Wouldn't it be a good idea if you were to go outside just till – well, till things are a bit more – normal? I mean, well, sir, it can't go on like this for long." The animal lolloped up to Specs and sniffed at the socks he'd put on for the party – screaming yellow they were – and I think they frightened it because suddenly it beat it for the back of the sofa, and wouldn't budge. "Oh, come on out you brute – I mean, sir," said Specs, and prodded at it, but the rabbit scratched out at us and we couldn't make it move. "All right," said Specs, when he was we weren't getting any co-operation, "all right, if that's where you want to be you'll jolly well have to stay there." And he got the big wastepaper basket, and with a bit of skilful manoeuvring put it over the rabbit's head and anchored it down with a couple of heavy books. "There! That'll fix you – I mean, you'll be all right now, sir," he said; "sorry, was that your paw?" And then he said to me, "That'll keep him quiet if anyone does come in, and now we must go and hunt up some lettuce and try to coax him into the garden with them. He's bound to come out for a lettuce."

So we hopped out through the French window to look for lettuces. I must say I felt a bit queer going off and leaving Mr Olivers cooped up underneath his own wastepaper basket, but it seemed the only reasonable thing to do.

It took us a little while finding a lettuce bed, but in the end we found one, and yanked a lettuce up in each hand and came tearing back across the garden. The children hadn't come in from the dining-room yet – we could hear them squabbling away over the crackers. We fairly leapt in at the window, hoping to be in time, and – there was Mr Olivers, standing beside the sofa, just picking a few white hairs off the leg of his trousers!

We just stood there and gaped, and the soil dripped off the roots of our lettuces on to Mrs Olivers' drawing-room carpet. I don't know when I've felt such a fool. "Where in the world have you been?" Mr Olivers asked, "and what do you think you're doing with those lettuces?" There just wasn't any answer. How were we to know the magic would wear off so soon? We mumbled something about a new game, and Specs took the lettuces and threw them out of the window, and we started to scrape up the mud off the floor. Just then the party burst in on us and they all started to climb on our backs, and I never thought I'd have been so glad to see the little dears again!

We didn't stay for the conjuror. Somehow we didn't feel we could. We excused ourselves because of some prep that needn't really have been done that night at all, and thanked Mrs Olivers for the lovely afternoon. We thanked Mr Olivers too. He looked at us in a puzzled sort of way. "I don't like the colour of those socks, McCann," was all he said.

It was in the art class about a fortnight afterwards that the odd thing happened. Specs had been painting a really super abstract, all different shades of green it was, and then he painted across one corner of it the shape of a rabbit's head, just the silhouette, as clear as could be, only in tomato colour. Mr Olivers was coming round the room, looking at people's pictures. He stopped beside Specs. "Yes, McCann," he said, "I like that; it shows courage." Believe me, it did! "Do you really like it, sir?" asked Specs, looking all pleased and eager, "do you think it is – significant?" "Yes, I do," Mr Olivers said, with a queer faraway look in his eye, as if he were trying to remember something, "very significant, McCann." And he stared at the picture and then at Specs and back at the picture again. He put a hand up and scratched the back of his ear. "Very significant, McCann."

"I thought so myself, sir," said Specs, and he painted in a whisker.

6

Giving the Bird the Bird

Specs was unlucky this term, he got 'flu all by himself, when everybody else had finished with it. Now 'flu can be quite a sociable business – after the first few days – if you have it along with everybody else, and the classrooms get emptier and emptier while the san gets fuller and fuller. It's fun to lie in bed talking and eating oranges when you should be doing Latin prose, or maths tests, and to shout, "Bring In Your Dead!" every time the nurses arrive with a new patient; we used to have bets who would be the next to get it. But Specs waited till everyone else had had it, and the nurses up at the san had just had a thorough purge and gone off on holiday. So Matron had him all to herself, and wasn't she pleased? Matron simply pines away when she hasn't any invalids, so she welcomed Specs with open arms. Poor old Specs! While he really was ill he was jolly glad to have her, for she's a wizard with iced drinks and crumpled pillows, and she read to him by the hour when his eyes were too sore for him to read. But once he was tottering around again he just couldn't throw her off. She followed him about with a thermometer and a few extra scarves, and he couldn't exactly be rude to her because she'd been such an angel before.

Even when he was back at school Specs had to be off games for a fortnight, and when the rest of us were down at the games field he didn't know how to put in his time. If he found a book to read and went up to the dorm Matron would hound him out for some fresh air, and if he went out she would swaddle him up and tell him to keep moving but not to get too hot, and as Specs was much too hot before he'd even started moving at all this wasn't exactly easy to do.

Then I got my wrist twisted in a bit of a scrap up in the dorm one night, and I was off games too. Sprained wrists aren't a bit interesting, so Matron wasn't really much concerned with me, but Specs was still her chief joy, and he was getting desperate. I suppose it was the 'flu, but he didn't seem able to snap out of things at all, and I could see that the more Matron fussed about him the more he fussed about himself. I watched him one day taking his pulse in an algebra class, and he started nipping into the gym to weigh himself when we were coming in from break. So one games afternoon I asked my father – he's the headmaster – if Specs and I could have leave to go to the zoo, and I don't think he can have been listening to me properly, because he said yes, we could.

It took us a bit of a time getting there, and then we were held up at the turnstile while Specs and the man had an argument about whether he was a child or an adult. Specs ducked down to show the man he was wearing a school cap, but the man seemed to think this was a disguise or something – Specs had grown yards this term, all of a sudden – and in the end Specs had to pay a bob while I got in for threepence. Anyway, Specs said that to have an afternoon away from Matron was cheap even at the price.

The animals had mostly been fed, so they were lying around with their backs to us, digesting, and they weren't a bit interested. But at the far end beyond the reptile house there was a little enclosure that looked to us to be new, and we went along to see what was in it. At first it seemed to be empty, and then Specs gave a most awful gasp, and pointed, and said, "Good heavens! Look – it's her – it's Matron!"

Right enough it was awfully like her; it was a long thin bird and it poked its head forwards as it walked, and set its feet down all of a piece at right angles to each other, just like Matron does. There was a bunch of white feathers on its head, just like the frilly cap she wears, and it had round serious eyes, like Matron when she's looking at the rash on your chest and making up her mind which kind it is. Best of all the bird cocked its head at us and twittered softly to itself, and this is what Matron does while she's thinking. I thought it was awfully funny, but Specs was a bit shattered by the shock – it really was most fearfully like Matron. He turned quite pale, I thought, though whether it was the 'flu or the bird that did it I wasn't sure. Then all of a sudden the bird fixed its eyes on Specs and started to run towards where we were standing, making the queerest throaty clucking and stretching its long neck out. Specs stepped away from the wire and fell over backwards, but his cap was jerked off his head and it sailed over and fell at the bird's feet. There's always a wind up there, and I told you Specs has grown a lot.

51

I went on laughing for quite a while before I noticed that Specs was really bothered about it. "It was a new cap," he said, "and she'll be lepping mad if I go back in my bare head." I stopped laughing; it wasn't like Specs not to see how funny it all was. "Anyway, maybe I should have a cap on," he growled. This shook me. "We'll get it back, don't you worry," I said. "How?" he asked, glaring at me, and I hadn't any good answer ready. Specs generally has all the good ideas but I suppose the 'flu had washed them all out. "Think of something, for goodness sake," he said, so I thought. It wasn't easy, for there was nobody in sight at that end of the zoo, and the bird was stirring the cap around with its beak by now – looking for the name tape, I expect – so that if we didn't get it back pretty soon it wouldn't be worth getting back at all.

At last I had a kind of an idea, and I told Specs about it. There was a tree beside the wire, and Specs could climb it and drop down into the enclosure and get the cap that way, and while he was getting it I would go round to the other side of the wire and keep the bird distracted over there. It wasn't much of a plan, and Specs said so, but it seemed the best thing we could think up, so we decided to try it.

At first I couldn't attract the bird over to my end of the enclosure at all. She gave me a vague look or two, but then gazed fondly back at Specs and went on playing with his cap. Meanwhile Specs got up into the tree – very slowly and carefully, poor old Specs – ready to get over when the chance came. I was nearly giving up hope by this time of getting the wretched bird to take any notice of me, and at last I made a face at it, and stuck out my tongue. That worked the trick. When the bird saw me with my tongue out she came lepping over to my side of the wire, really interested, just like Matron, and Specs dropped down and grabbed the cap. But he made a good thud when he landed and the bird heard him. She wheeled around, and then made for him, half flying, half running with her neck stretched out, and those queer noises in her throat again, only louder than ever.

Specs never moved. I thought at the time he was being most awfully brave, but he said afterwards he was feeling very queer after jumping down off the tree, and he couldn't have turned and run if he'd been paid. Actually there wasn't the slightest need for him to run. The bird stopped when she got to him, and put her head on one side and twittered at him very lovingly with her large eyes fixed on his face. When Specs saw she wasn't going to hurt him he started moving to the side of the wire again. But then we discovered the really bad part of my plan. There were no trees inside the enclosure to give Specs a leg up on the way back. He had got his cap all right, but he couldn't get out of the wire.

Specs stood there telling me just what he thought of my plan, while the bird rubbed her silly head against his shoulder and crooned at him.

I was just going to go off to look for one of the keepers to explain what had happened and make the best story I could out of it when I saw a man coming up the path towards the enclosure with a wheelbarrow. I signed to Specs to hide, and he got round the far side of a kind of shed place, where I suppose the bird slept, and crouched down, and the bird followed him. The man with the wheelbarrow unlocked the gate and took the barrow in. There was food of some kind in it, and he stopped wheeling it just inside the gate and looked around. The bird, of course, was out of sight, so was Specs, so the man lifted a big box from the barrow and went over to a trough, leaving the gate open behind him. I dashed round to the far side of the wire to tell this to Specs. He was having his own troubles, because a little boy had just come along and was looking at him and the bird very excitedly, and calling to his mother to "Come and see." I told the kid that if he didn't hurry up he'd miss the elephant having its dinner, and when he had scuttled away to round up his mother and look for the elephant I explained to Specs about the man and the barrow. So Specs took a look round the corner of the shed, and the man was still busy scraping the trough out before he filled it, so Specs stuffed the remains of his cap in his pocket – it was too muddy to put on – and started off for the open gate. He was about half way across when a little cart drawn by a donkey came up the path and stopped. It was driven by one of the keepers. Specs did something on the spur of the moment which I thought at the time was very clever of him, though afterwards I wasn't so sure. He picked up the wheelbarrow and wheeled it out through the gate, just as if he'd been on the job. The keeper in the cart evidently thought he was. "Here," he called, "take a load of this along to the monkeys, will you," and he shovelled a heap of chopped-up greens on to the barrow, jerked up his donkey and trotted off.

Specs stared after him, and then decided that he'd better see the thing through, and he started off for the monkey house, only too thankful that it wasn't the lions' dinner he had been asked to deliver. I started to go after him, and then I stopped dead and turned round. I was being followed too. It was the bird! Specs hadn't noticed that she had run after him when he picked up the wheelbarrow, and as he didn't stop to pull the door closed when he went out, she had slipped out after him, and was padding along behind us now, panting a little and talking to herself in an undertone of anxious twitterings, just like Matron does.

Specs didn't know we were being followed until he noticed people on the path stopping to stare, and children running alongside, pointing and laughing. I shall never forget his face when he did turn round. If looks could have killed, that twittering fowl would have twittered her last. But she stopped a few feet away and cocked her head on one side, and looked at him fondly out of her big round eyes, as if apologising for her devotion. Specs gave her one look, and then shrugged his shoulders, turned to the barrow again, and started to wheel it at a furious pace, without another backward glance.

We had collected quite a following by the time we reached the monkey house. Specs parked the wheelbarrow just inside the door, and then we cut and ran. We had cleared the crowd by the time we came to the lion house, and we spent a long time in there, getting our breath back. We had just made up our minds to get going when the bird popped her long neck in through the door, as if she wondered what was keeping us. We wheeled around and made for the other door, and ran to the elephant house without looking behind us. But could we throw that bird off? No, she was waiting for us when we came out, and she followed us all the way to the house where the rabbits and their families are, and although we kicked our heels there for quite a while she was there when we came out, and so were quite a lot of the original crowd, who had spotted the bird and become interested again. But among them was an important-looking keeper who didn't seem too pleased. "Now then young fellow, what's all this about?" he said to Specs, as we came out into the sunshine and the bird welcomed us as if we'd been away for a month, "what do you think you are doing with that bird?"

"I am attempting to hand it over to the proper authority," said Specs, rather grandly. "It seems to have escaped – one of your men must have slipped up somewhere." The keeper seemed quite impressed at that, and he asked Specs if he would keep the bird for a minute to two, which was about the only thing Specs could have done with it. Then the keeper went away and came back very soon with four other men, carrying a kind of outsize in hen coops.

So that was the end of the poor bird's excursion. In spite of a lot of squawking and flapping she was hustled into the box, and the last we saw of her she was gazing mournfully out through the bars, making desolate clucking noises at Specs. I almost felt sorry for her; she was evidently feeling it very much.

We turned and beat it for the Exit and climbed on the first bus going our way. Specs didn't talk much on the trip back to school; he seemed to be brooding, and I was quite worried.

When we turned in at the gate the first person we

saw was Matron. When she spotted Specs she began twittering gladly and ambled up with her large eyes all full of affection and reproach. "So there you are, McCann," she said, "and without your cap too. You really are a bad lad – do you expect me to follow you about all afternoon?"

I don't suppose Matron will ever know why Specs gave that sudden hoot of laughter and ran off into the house and upstairs two at a time to the dorm. She looked at me, and I looked at her, and she made a mournful clucking noise, and then I muttered some kind of an excuse or other, and went after Specs. He was sitting on his bed laughing till I thought he really would hurt himself. I was so relieved that I sat down on the bed as well, and we laughed until we were so sore we had to stop.

But Specs was cured from that day. I think Matron knew she had lost her grip because she didn't pollute him any more, and luckily Blenkinsop developed an appendix that night, so the rest of us were small beans till the end of term.

7

For Services Rendered

Of all the masters at school Mr Jenkins – we call him the Droner – is the hardest to listen to. He teaches Latin, which may have something to do with it, and last term he invented a new thing called Classical General Knowledge, for one period in the week. This was a dreary kind of lecture, and after he had finished we had to write an essay about it for homework, but as we all had little books about it anyway it wasn't hard to mug it up. But it was hard to sit there and be droned at. The Droner had only three notes in his voice and two of them were the same. He used to get wild if we fidgeted, so Specs McCann invented a way of putting in the time. It was a kind of yoga, like they do in India. You had to open your eyes a little bit wider than usual and stare at the tip of the Droner's nose. Then you emptied your mind of everything, and if you were lucky you went deaf, quite deaf. What with remembering to keep your mind a blank and your eyes on the Droner's nose, it was surprising how soon the bell went. Specs got quite good at this after a bit of practice, and the best of it was he looked as if he was simply lapping up every word. Some of the chaps laughed, of course, and said it was easier for some people to empty their minds than for others, but I think myself they were just jealous.

There was one afternoon last term when the Droner's Classical General Knowledge Lecture was so dry you could have struck a match on it. There was a stray bee buzzing about inside the window too, and between the pair of them it made you want to stamp about and throw things. All about the Campus Martius, it was, the Field of Mars, where the Roman youths used to hold their games and Athletic Sports. There was a little plaster statue of a head of Mars on the bookcase in our class, and the Droner set it up on the desk in front of him. I had stopped listening to him, and was watching Specs. He had given up the yoga business after the first ten minutes, and now he was trying out another idea we had invented for sitting still. You put your feet very flat on the floor, and your hands palm upward under your desk. Then you pressed hard with your hands and feet at the same time, and if you had very good balance – and enough books piled on your desk – you could lift yourself off your chair about half an inch, though it looked as if you were still sitting down. It took quite a lot of effort to do this, and Specs was getting red in the face when all at once the desk flew up (he hadn't put enough books on it, silly ass) and scattered his belongings all round the place.

This was a diversion, anyway, and it took the Droner about three minutes to tell Specs what he thought of him. I felt sorry for Specs really, because the inkwell had hit him on the nose. Luckily it was empty, but it made his nose bleed.

The Droner felt a lot better after this, and started in on Mars again with terrific energy, as if it was the nine o'clock news. By this time we were getting desperate, for Specs's nose didn't bleed for long, and when even the interest of that had died down there were still ten long minutes to go to the end of class. You see there was a match that afternoon, the first of the season's Form Matches, and we had drawn the Upper Fourth. Of course they were bigger chap than us, but we had a pretty good eleven, and meant to put up a jolly fine show. The Upper Fourth had a free period during our Classical General Knowledge lecture, and we could hear the smack of the ball down at the nets, where they were putting in a bit of practice. Sitting still became quite impossible. So Specs did a very silly thing – he put a piece of chocolate in his cheek and started chewing. Now the Droner can detect a moving jaw at a hundred yards. He spotted Specs at once, and that was that. We were to stay in after the class – me as well as Specs because I stuck in a good word about Specs's nose being hurt – and copy out some Caesar.

"Oh, and McCann," said Droner, "you haven't any of that chocolate left, have you?"

"Yes, thank you, sir," said Specs, and this made the Droner madder than ever.

"Well now, let me see," he said. "Wasn't there some little matter of a match this afternoon – a combat on the Campus Martius?" And he laughed at his little joke.

"Well, actually sir, it's in the lower field, sir," said Specs, without a smile.

The Droner likes people to notice his jokes. He smiled toothily. "Don't you think, McCann, seeing you are unhappily prevented from attending the match in person you could at least make some little contribution to the success of your team, some sacrifice, shall we say?" He looked down at the statue of the head of Mars. "Ah yes, I have it, of course. The rest of that chocolate, McCann, it would do nicely, don't you think, for an offering to Mars to bring success to your fellows. A good idea to lay it at his feet, don't you think?"

"I see what you mean, sir, although he hasn't any feet," Specs agreed solemnly, looking at the statue which only came down as far as the shoulders of Mars, but he took the rest of the chocolate out of his pocket and laid it down before the statue respectfully; then he stepped back and raised his hand in a Roman salute (we did Julius Caesar last term).

Of course the class laughed, and I think the Droner would have done something really desperate then if the bell hadn't gone: anyway he just scooped his gown up round him and beat it.

The rest of the class beat it too, and Specs and I were left. "You were a poor fool to go sticking your nose in," Specs said to me, which was his way of saying thank you, and we opened our Caesars and started to write the beastly stuff out.

It was hard to concentrate because we could hear shouts and clapping every now and then from the cricket field. But we scraped away at old Caesar until we got into a kind of miserable daze, what with the heat and the dreariness of it all.

Then suddenly we heard the chaps coming back, and a couple of them put their heads round the door, grinning like mad, and said that we had won. The Upper

Fourth had gone down like a pack of cards, and we'd had no trouble putting up the necessary runs. That fairly woke us up, and we did a kind of samba round the room. Briggs (our fast bowler) came in with half a dozen people hanging on to him clapping him on the back. "Good old Briggs," they shouted, "you had them cold."

"What about me?" asked Specs, doing a bit of fancy footwork along the windowsill.

"You!" they shouted, "much good you did us!"

"What about Mars, then?" asked Specs, and he did a couple of high kicks across the floor to the desk where the statue was standing, "he fixed it up for you, didn't you, Mars old boy?"

And then he stopped with one foot in the air and his mouth open, because – the chocolate had gone! There wasn't a sign of it. Specs looked so funny the chaps began to laugh and said of course we'd eaten it, and when we swore we hadn't they said then somebody had been in and boned it while we'd been slogging away at our Caesar. Specs and I looked at each other and we said nothing at the time. But after the classroom had cleared again we looked all round the desk and under the blotting-paper, but there wasn't a sign of it. We both knew quite well that nobody had taken it because just before the others had come in Specs had gone up to the desk to fill his pen, and the chocolate was still there then. And now it had gone.

Luckily the Droner must have forgotten all about it, so no enquiries were made, and that was how the whole affair started. And although Specs and I didn't talk about it much at the start, and never said a word to the other chaps, we both thought about it quite a lot.

The Wednesday after that was the first of the inter-form tennis matches, and we had drawn the Science Fourth. We didn't really expect to win because we had a rotten team – you can judge how rotten when you know that Specs and I were both in it – but nobody thinks much of tennis at school anyway. It was a lovely afternoon, and as soon as classes were over everyone rushed out to the courts. Specs was a bit slow putting his books away (maybe it was just an accident) and I waited for him. We were just going out of the classroom when he stuck his hand in his pocket and pulled out a packet of liquorice allsorts. "Here you are, old chap," he said, laughing in rather a silly way, "this'll keep you chewing." And he chucked it on to the desk.

Whether I was thinking so hard about what Specs had done that I forgot to be nervous I don't know, but we both played better tennis that day than we ever did before or since. We just couldn't do anything wrong. I felt as if there was something inside me taking charge, and Specs told me afterwards that was how he felt too. Anyhow we won our match in a couple of easy sets, and then found that the rest of our team were doing just as well, and the whole thing was a walk-over for us.

After the excitement had died down we walked back to school, and I couldn't help wondering what Specs would do. He didn't seem excited or anything, but as we were going past the classroom he said, casual-like, "I could do with a sweet, couldn't you?" and we turned in and went up to the desk.

There were no sweets there. We looked at the empty desk, and we looked at the statue of Mars, and I thought myself he seemed a bit smug, almost as if he'd just finished licking his lips. Specs took a deep breath, and then he said, "Ah well, I suppose it's all in a good cause," and he turned round and went out of the classroom whistling between his teeth. That's Specs all over.

After that things began to happen in earnest. It seemed that the Lower Fourth – that's us – were unbeatable. We never had a season like it. We won the fives and we won the tennis, and little by little – no one was more surprised than ourselves – we worked our way through the cricket championship (which was the biggest concern of any) till we reached the semifinal. Specs was really excited by now, and he didn't pretend he wasn't. "Do you think," he said to me the day before, "do you think peppermints or more chocolate?"

"What about coconut ice?" I suggested, "they've got some in the tuck shop, but it won't last long – everybody's after it."

"Bit expensive," Specs grumbled, "and it's getting near the end of term. Don't you think peppermints would do all right? That was how we won the fives."

"Yes, but we only just won," I reminded him, "better have the coconut ice and make sure. I'll pay it all if you haven't enough."

We got the coconut ice from the tuck shop, and Mars must have liked it because to everybody's astonishment we beat the Remove in the semifinal of the cricket.

That meant we were to play the Lower Fifth in the final. It had never been heard of before, the Lower Fourth getting into the cricket final, and it was the talk of the school.

Then the awful thing happened. Some ass threw a stone at the tuck shop window and broke it, and there was a fearful row because nobody owned up, and the whole school was gated from the tuck shop for a week. Everybody went about feeling hungry and moaning and lamenting, but of course, Specs and I had a lot more to moan and lament about than they had.

Then I had a bright idea. "Look here," I said, "why must it be sweets? Couldn't it be money? You got half a crown from your uncle on Sunday. Have you spent it?"

"No, I was keeping it to celebrate with afterwards," Specs said, "but maybe it *would* do the trick," and we both agreed it was worth trying, anyway.

I must say I admired Specs the way he put down the half-crown in front of the statue, and even saluted it like he did the first day. I for one wouldn't have blamed him if he'd asked for change and just put down a shilling.

But from the beginning of the match we knew in our hearts that the half-crown wasn't going to do the trick. Our bowling soon went to bits and the Lower Fifth started to hit us about and piled up a big score before we managed to get them out. Specs looked worried – after all, it was half a crown. But after the tea interval our side pulled up their socks a little and managed to stay in long enough to make it a draw. "Ah well," Specs said, "better than nothing," and when we'd finished clapping our team, we went up to school. I knew what Specs was after, and I slipped away from the others and followed him into the classroom. It was getting dark by this time, and at first I thought the desk in front of the statue was empty, but then Specs put out his hand and picked something up. "There's something here, anyway," he said, in rather a queer voice, and he brought it over to the light.

It was a coin, but not an ordinary coin, not a coin we knew, and it was made of something like brass, and it had a design like a bird on one side and a man's head on the other. You couldn't really see the markings because it was rubbed so smooth, as if ever so many hands had rubbed it through ever so many years. There were some capital letters too, but they were too faint to read.

Specs whistled and passed the coin to me, and it felt odd in my hand and unfamiliar, and I gave it quickly back to Specs who wrapped it in a corner of his hankie and tied a knot on it.

Mr Jenkins was taking prep that evening, and after it was over Specs went up to the desk and I followed him. "Excuse me, sir," he said, "but could you please tell me anything about – about this coin?" and he pulled out his hankie, untied the knot, and laid the coin on the desk.

The Droner picked it up carefully – he's always a little on the careful side with Specs, in case it's a leg-pull – and he squinted at it down his nose. Then he gave the least bit of a start. "This is a Roman coin, McCann, or at least I should say it is very like a Roman coin – a good copy, yes, quite a creditable copy." But we both knew he knew it wasn't a copy. "How much would it be worth," asked Specs, trying to keep his voice level, "in present-day money, I mean?" The Droner hummed and hawed, and went into a long technical chat which didn't seem to be getting us anywhere. In the end he said he thought it might be worth a shilling or a little more. "About one and threepence?" said Specs, and his voice shook the least little bit. "Just about," the Droner agreed, "where did you come across it, McCann?"

"It was given to me in change," said Specs, in a queer voice, and he took the coin quickly and tied it up in the hankie again. The Droner made him promise to let him see it again by daylight, and Specs said he would.

But the next day although the knot was still in the hankie the coin wasn't. It had simply gone. We looked for it everywhere. The Droner asked Specs to show it to him, and Specs had to own up it was lost. The Droner smiled rather a nasty smile and said: "It certainly was a very creditable imitation," and we had to leave it at that.

When we came back at the beginning of this term we found we'd both been saving up our spare cash for the football season, and we were quite rolling. But when we went into the classroom the statue wasn't there – one of the cleaners had knocked it down in the holidays and broken it. So that was that – in the meantime, anyway. You don't know anyone who wants to sell a small statue of Mars, do you?

8

A Question of Gravity

Specs was having a run of bad luck at the beginning of this term. You know how it is at school, when one thing goes wrong it seems hard for anything to go right. He started off badly, of course. We had unpacked our trunks on the first day and were taking them along to the boxroom when Specs had the brilliant idea of punting them along with cricket bats. The passage from our dorm to the boxroom is long and shiny, and with a good shove off we managed to get up quite a speed. Specs was doing a good ten knots, singing a gondolier's song at the top of his voice when Matron came along with a stack of sheets and a bottle of marking ink. Matron wasn't hurt, but – well, there was an awful lot of marking ink in that bottle.

To get through the lines he was set for this, Specs risked leaving his Latin translation unprepared, and then of course the Droner chose him out next day, and gave Specs another set of lines because it was obvious he hadn't looked at the thing. So it went on, one set of lines leading to another. I was worried about Specs because it was getting him down. He almost expected the lines before he got them. I tried to copy his handwriting, but I was no use at it, and we decided it wasn't worth the risk.

One morning when we were waiting for Mr Hughes to come in to take French class, Specs was busy mugging up some science. He hadn't been able to do it before because he'd spent all prep time doing extra arithmetic because he hadn't had time to learn his geometry, because of some lines he was writing for not knowing his French. You get the idea, don't you? "Every particle of matter in the universe," muttered Specs, "every particle of matter in the universe attracts every other particle with a force which depends on their masses and distance apart." It was Newton's universal law of gravitation, and a pretty dead cert for the science class. "Every particle of matter in the universe," said Specs again, "attracts every other particle." Then he stopped and looked at me. "Gosh!" he said, "can't say I feel the attraction myself." I let this pass, and he went on learning. "What a lot of nonsense," he said, "calling this a scientific law; it's just plain sense." "Still," I said, "it was jolly clever of old Newton to spot it." "Clever, my eye," Specs snarled, "it only means what goes up must come down. Lot of fancy chat about very little, if you ask me." I hadn't asked him, but I didn't say so. "What good does it do anyway?" he grumbled on. Then he lifted his hand in the air, and declaimed solemnly, "I hereby denounce the works and faith of Sir Isaac Newton," and while I was thinking out the answer to this one, the door opened, and in came Mr Hughes to take the French class. Mr Hughes is a new master who wears shiny brown shoes and bright yellow ties, and his wife is a smasher. I must say he's brightened French classes up a lot. He tells funny stories and makes puns, and if you don't understand a little French you miss the laughs, so chaps find themselves learning without meaning to. There were a good many laughs this morning, but Specs seemed to be missing them. He was sitting as solemn as an owl, with such a strange look on his face, an inward look, like when you've swallowed too much ice cream. Then I noticed him very quickly put his hands down under the seat of his chair and hold on. He put up first one hand and then the other very carefully and rubbed his ears, and shook his head a little, and then held on to his desk again. Just at that moment Mr Hughes came out with a specially funny story, and everybody laughed, and I was glad to see Specs was laughing too. But when everybody else had finished laughing Specs went on. First it was a giggle, rather an uncertain one, then a hinney, and then a real cackle. Mr Hughes looked over at Specs inquiringly. It hadn't really been as funny as all that. "Now, McCann," said Mr Hughes, "joke over." But Specs laughed on. He put his hand in his pocket for his hankie, still holding on to the seat of his desk with the other. "McCann, control yourself," Mr Hughes snapped, the smile wiped right off his face. Specs stuffed the hankie into his mouth, but he was still roaring with laughter and quite red in the face. "What is the matter with you, boy?" barked Mr Hughes. "Have you completely lost your sense of gravity?" This was the finishing touch. Specs pulled his hankie out of his mouth like a streamer and burst into the wildest hoot of laughter I ever heard. He tried to speak, but he choked instead, and the tears streamed down his face. Mr Hughes saw things were out of control. "Take your friend away till he recovers himself," he said to me, "and then I'll give him some French verbs to sober him up." Specs was coughing and choking by now, so I grabbed him and got him out of the classroom into the passage. He hung on to my arm on the way out, and when we were in the passage he grabbed hold of a radiator and began to get his breath back.

"What on earth is the joke?" I asked, really peeved because he'd made such a fool of himself. And then, in between gasps and wheezes of laughter, Specs told me. He really *had* lost his sense of gravity. As soon as he had denounced Newton and his theory of gravitation he began to have a peculiar tickling in his ears and to feel very light. He found he was bobbing up and down on the seat of the desk, hardly touching it. And then, to his horror he found he was off the desk altogether, not sitting down at all, but just held down a few inches in the air, by his knees which were tucked under the desk in front. Even then he felt his knees were slipping, and he grabbed the seat to keep himself from floating off altogether. He remembered our science master had said our sense of gravity was due to semicircular canals in the ears, so he knew what had happened. So of course he began to laugh, and then Mr Hughes's question was the last straw. No wonder he had laughed. The two of us sat on the radiator now and laughed till it hurt. Nobody came along, which was just as well, because all of a sudden Specs forgot, and let go of the radiator, and then of course there was nothing to keep him down and he went wobbling up towards the ceiling. He looked so silly, flapping his hands and feet, and his mouth open like a fish, that I only just remembered in time and

71

tackled him round the knees and pulled him down. This sobered him up, and we went along to the cloakroom to think things over. It wasn't too easy getting there, because I had to hold Specs down on to the floor. He kept bobbing up like a cork between steps, and he said it felt like trying to walk under water at the deep end of the baths.

We had only a few minutes before classes ended, and the chaps would be coming down for break, so we hadn't much time to think. Specs took off one of his shoes and dropped it, and it fell on to the floor all right, so we knew it was only Specs and not his clothes that wouldn't stay down. That gave us an idea, and we decided to put all the heavy things we could into Specs's pockets and see if they would do the trick. So I left Specs in the cloakroom and scrounged around in the bicycle shed and collected a couple of monkey wrenches, and then I went along to the boiler-house and filled my hankie full of chunks of clinker from the dump where George, the handyman, had been clearing out the boiler. I raced back to the cloakroom and was just in time to stow the stuff in Specs's pockets before the bell went and the other chaps came in. "You were an ass, Specs," said Wilkes, "you didn't half look silly, braying away like that." Specs got red and forgot about holding on to the seat and stood up, and I was scared he would do his Peter Pan stunt again, but luckily the stuff we had put in his pockets seemed to be just enough to keep him on the floor, and he stood there rocking a little and bobbing up and down with anger, threatening to punch Wilkes's nose. However, before it could develop into anything one of the prefects came in to clear the cloakroom, and I took Specs firmly by the arm and walked him out. We went round to the boiler-house and stoked up with anthracite until Specs decided he had enough ballast in and could move about all right. On the way back to school we ran into Matron, and she said, "McCann, what have you got in your pockets? You'll ruin the shape of your clothes. Empty them out." Specs growled, "Sorry, Matron – afterwards – must go now – late for class," and we bolted, but after school was over we found a safe spot at the bottom of the garden to talk it over.

The odd thing was that Specs seemed to take it all very cheerfully. I suppose he was really a bit light-headed. However, in the end I made him see how serious it all was. With Matron on the prowl loading his pockets was no good, so I left Specs under some bushes and went off to look for something better. George's workshop was lying open, and I went in and found a couple of pieces of lead piping and some light wire, and lugged the stuff back to Specs.

But he wasn't there! His coat was lying on the ground, but there was no sign of Specs. Then I heard a noise up above me, and I looked up. There was Specs in his shirt-sleeves halfway up a tree, grinning down at me like a monkey. "What in the world are you doing up there?" I shouted. "I couldn't help it," he yelled back, "you were such an age and it was so gorgeous and hot I took off my coat and the first thing I knew I was hitting the branches. I just floated up." "Well, you can just float down now and see what uncle's brought you," I called. "I don't want to come down," Specs said happily, "it's wizard up here – 'There are fairies at the bottom of our garden'," and he bobbed about up at the top of the tree. "Take care," I called, "you'll fall." Specs laughed like anything at this. "I couldn't if I tried," he said, and let go with both hands to show me. Instead of falling he rose, and had only just time to catch hold of the very last of the branches, or he would have floated off into space. "Where do you think you're going?" I yelled. "You come down out of that." So down he came, carefully handling his way from branch to branch. I think he'd really got a fright, and we rigged up the lead piping with the wire, fastening two pieces of it on to his braces, so that they hung down inside his trouser legs. "I hope I don't clank when I walk," said Specs, but he tried it, and he didn't.

For five days Specs went around like that. He didn't look any different, except that he walked a bit stiffly. We were thankful if wasn't the winter because I don't know how he could have stowed the lead piping away under his rugger togs. Having a bath was a bit awkward, but Specs found the water helped to keep him down, and he hooked his toes in under the taps and didn't wash very much.

Specs was full of ideas about the Sports. He has always been pretty good at jumping, and of course now the high jump would be all his own – provided he could come down again after he'd cleared the bar. He meant to practise with weights in his shoes till he got the right weight to bring him down again, and intended to have a rope tied round him while we were experimenting, so that I could hold the other end and haul him down again if the weight hadn't been quite heavy enough.

However, it never came to that. I don't know if walking around with lead piping slung on to his legs made Specs tired, or what it was. He was never any good at getting up in the morning anyway, and since this happened he'd nabbed a couple of extra blankets, because the weight of them kept him down in the bed. One morning when the bell went Specs didn't stir, so I thumped him till he grunted and opened his eyes, and then I went off to ask Matron for some clean socks because all the heel seemed to have melted off one of mine overnight. Matron was busy taking Potter's temperature, and by the time I had got my socks the second bell was ringing, and the chaps were going downstairs. But when I went into the dorm there was Specs still asleep. I shouted at him and shook him, but all he did was let out a snore like a volcano opening up, and then he smiled gently and rubbed his nose. I heard the prefect coming along the passage to see if all the dormitories were clear. He popped in next door. "All away?" he asked, and nobody answered. I shook Specs for all I was worth. The prefect (it was long Peters) stuck his head round our door. "All away?" he said. Then he saw Specs. "Is McCann never up yet? Lazy hound!" He came over and took hold of the bedclothes and yanked them right off the bed. At first Specs didn't stir, but just lay there in his blue striped pyjamas and snored. Then, quite slowly and rather beautifully he rose in the air, off the bed, and drifted, still sound asleep, up to the ceiling. Long Peters let a screech out of him, and passed out on to the floor. This did wake Specs and he shivered and felt for the bedclothes, and then opened his eyes and stared down at me, trying to remember where he was and what he was doing up there. I got on to the end of the bed and stretched up my hand and he took hold of it, so that I was able to pull him down. He held on to the end of the bed and I threw his clothes at him. "Get a move on," I said, and turned to see how long Peters was. He was just coming round, and I got a face cloth and wet his forehead and asked if he was feeling better. He opened his eyes and stared round, and then he saw Specs who was nearly dressed by this time. "What in the world," he said, giving a little gasp, "what in the world was McCann doing up there?" "Up where?" I said. "He's getting dressed." "But – but –" stammered long Peters, and he gaped at the ceiling, with his mouth open like a fish. "I say," said Specs, tying his tie and flattening down his hair, "have you been seeing things? You know, you don't look a bit well." Long Peters goggled for a while and Specs stayed with him while I went off to fetch Matron, so this gave us both the excuse we needed for being so late for breakfast.

I hadn't a chance to talk to Specs alone before school. It was science first lesson, and what did Mr Finch do but ask Specs right away to repeat Newton's universal law of gravitation. Specs brightened up at once, and got on his feet and recited, very loud and clear, "Every particle of matter in the universe attracts every other particle with a force which depends on their masses and distance apart." "Quite clear about that, McCann?" asked Mr Finch, looking at Specs down his beak, "no difficulty there, I hope."

"Oh none at all, sir, thank you, sir," said Specs, and sat down rather heavily and suddenly. I knew by that, and by his secret grin that his sense of gravity had come back. So when it came round to break we decided to nip down to the bike shed and get rid of the lead. But of course it was terribly heavy for him to walk with it now and, not being used to it, Specs tripped at the top of the stairs and fell down the flight. Mr Finch was going past at the bottom, with a stack of exercise books. He and the books were all spread out on top of Specs. I helped him up and gathered the books. He wasn't really hurt, and he's always a good sport. "McCann," he said, when he and Specs and the books were sorted out, "have you no respect for Sir Isaac Newton and his theory?" "Oh indeed I have, sir," said Specs, rubbing his shins and straightening his glasses, "it's a matter of the utmost gravity." That's the sort of fellow Specs is.

9

Specs and the Cuckoo Clock

Our form got studies this term instead of having to share a common room – that is to say there was a study for each pair of boys, so of course I was sharing one with Specs. In the holidays we had had a scrounge round for anything that might come in handy for furnishing our study, and between us we didn't do too badly. Specs did specially well because he played on his sisters' tender hearts by telling them how bare and spartan it all was at school, and by the time he'd finished they were nearly in tears and couldn't get to their knitting needles quick enough. I couldn't get away with this because I live at school anyway – my father's the headmaster. But Specs came back with his trunk stuffed with cushions – embroidered ones and knitted ones and crocheted ones – and we held an auction that fetched in a nice little balance and put the general opinion of Specs's sisters several points higher.

Our study looked so comfortable when we had finished fixing it up that people kept dropping in. It was quite the showplace in the corridor. We were afraid Tusky Russel would have beaten us when he staggered back from his first week-end at home with the head of a yak or something his uncle or someone had shot in Siberia or somewhere, but by the time he had fixed the beast up it filled half the study and there wasn't enough room to do any work. Then one of the maids nearly got her eye put out by its horn when she was sweeping, so Matron made Tusky take it home again at half-term.

One evening after this, when prep was over, we noticed nobody came in like they usually did, but there seemed to be great fun and games going on further along the corridor, so we went to see what it was all about. Tusky had brought back an electric clock. It was standing on the shelf in his study, very shiny and new, with a wide smug dial and the latest thing in numbers. And the study was full of people looking at it and listening to it – it didn't tick, of course, but if you put your ear down close it made a soft self-satisfied purr.

"Hallo," said Tusky when we came in, "you don't often favour us with the pleasure of your company." We knew what he meant by that – he and Specs were always scrapping, and Specs had taken to keeping out of his way to save trouble. "Nice clock you've got there," said Specs. "Yes, it's not bad," Tusky said, "come in any time you want to know the time, won't you? It'll be handy."

Of course it would be handy, that was the snag. The window of the common room we used to share looked straight across to the school clock, but in the study corridor there wasn't any way of telling the time except if you happened to have a watch, and generally watches stopped when you wanted them, or they all told different times and you had to work out an average, and by that time it was five minutes later. So of course everybody got into the habit of dropping into Tusky's study to see the time, and hardly anybody came to visit us any more.

Then one Saturday afternoon Specs said he had asked leave to go up to Belfast. He didn't say what he was going for, I don't think he really knew himself, all he said was, "There's still the money left over from the auction, so I had a kind of an idea." I couldn't go with him because we were having a choir rehearsal for the concert, but when I saw him coming into school just before evening call over with a parcel under his arm and a light in his eye I knew he'd got what he wanted. We didn't unwrap it till after supper when we'd got the study to ourselves – though we generally had it to ourselves nowadays anyway. "Now," said Specs, taking the last of the paper wrappings off like a mother peeling a shawl off a baby, "now, what do you think of that?"

Only Specs would have thought of it – it was a cuckoo clock! We stood and looked at it for a while in admiration. I suppose it was really the same as lots of other cuckoo clocks, a little wooden house with a clock face and hanging weights, and a very small pair of doors, but it was just the answer to Tusky Russel. Specs went and got a hammer and some nails and we fixed it up against the wall right away, and started it going. It was ticking away happily and busily and we were standing admiring it when Parkes from next door stuck his head in and said, "Aren't you coming down to prayers? Do you know what time it is?" "Of course we know, thanks," said Specs, nodding to the cuckoo clock. It wasn't really seven o'clock – the clock was a few minutes fast – but just at that moment the little doors flew open and the cuckoo said "Cuckoo!" very clearly and politely at us seven times, flapping its wings each time, and then went into its house again, and the doors closed.

Parkes stood there for a moment with his eyes goggling. Then he said "Gosh!" and went out, and we heard him running down the corridor and another door opening and shutting. "That should fix it," said Specs, beaming through his glasses, and he turned to the little clock. "Thank you, ma'am," he said.

It certainly did fix it. From that time on there was a constant stream of visitors at the study door, especially just before the hours. People stepped in to say "Hallo," and they stopped to make unnecessary conversation with one eye on the clock, and in the end the conversation just tailed off into nothing, and we stood around and gaped while the cuckoo did her stuff. Specs was awfully sorry when he had to be in class or at games, or even in bed when the cuckoo was due to come out. He used to stand there watching her with his head a little on one side and such a soppy look on his face he'd have laughed if he could have seen himself. He said she had great feeling, the bird, and I soon saw what he meant. When we had a lot of difficult prep she used to say "cuckoo" very softly and sympathetically, so as not to interrupt. On a wet Monday morning she used to say "cuckoo" shortly and crossly, and shut her door with an extra smart little snap, and when our form beat the Upper Fifth at cricket she "cuckooed" with such triumphant whoops that people came running in, and Specs declares she did one extra cuckoo, though as nobody had started counting at the beginning we couldn't be sure.

Now the worst of Specs is that when he gets worked up about something he gets very worked up about it, and can't think of anything else. The cuckoo in the cuckoo clock took him this way. He used to say "Hullo, ducks," when she came out – if there was nobody in the study, of course – and always "Thank you, ma'am," when she'd finished. Sometimes he would say "Perky to-day, isn't she?" or "I think she's feeling low," and he suggested we should come down from the dorm some night to see if she cuckooed at night in her sleep with her eyes shut, but I managed to get him put off that idea.

Then I came in late from a choir practice one evening and found the study door locked on the inside. I rattled the handle and told Specs to open up, and in a minute he did. "Come on in," he said, "and shut the door." His glasses were shining like searchlights, and he was walking about on tiptoe looking soppy, with one eye on the clock. It was ten to five and he wouldn't tell me what the excitement was. "Wait and you'll see for yourself," was all he would tell me, and as the hour came near I felt nearly as excited as he looked.

We stood on each side of the clock waiting while the last long endless minutes ticked past, and then at last the doors opened and the cuckoo said "cuckoo" five times and disappeared again. Specs turned to me. "Did you see it?" he whispered. I nodded – for the life of me I couldn't have spoken. Inside the little doors there was a small round white object. Our cuckoo had laid an egg.

Now it's all very well for you to say that I was soft, loony, loopy, crazy, barmy, nuts, anything you like, but you don't live with Specs like I do. He gets so earnest about things, and of course some very queer things have happened to him, haven't they, and you never know when they'll happen again.

It was quite impossible that a cuckoo in a cuckoo clock should lay an egg. I said this to Specs and he said rather haughtily, people should keep an open mind on things, and I said in this case his mind must be positively draughty, and we nearly had a row. But in the end he took it all so seriously that although I really didn't believe it myself, I didn't see why he shouldn't if he wanted to. And quite honestly I was a bit thrilled with it all myself.

I found out how Specs was taking the whole thing one day at dinner when I overheard him asking Mr Wilde, that's the new French master, how long it took a cuckoo's egg to hatch out. Mr Wilde is frightfully keen on birds – if you can get him sidetracked you needn't do any French for most of a period and he knows all the Lesser Spotted What Nots in Co. Down by their christian names. The question seemed to surprise him rather, and they went off to his room together to look at books. Specs didn't tell me what he'd said, but I found he'd put a big red ring round a date two Thursdays away, so I knew we hadn't long to wait.

On the Wednesday before the fateful Thursday, Specs hunted around in the study and took one of his sisters' cushion covers that nobody had bought at the auction, and hung it over the front like a curtain. Just as he was doing this Tusky came in for something – he'd been round quite a few times recently, I'd noticed – and when he saw the cushion cover hanging on the clock he grinned and said, "Broody, is she?" and Specs didn't say anything, but got rid of him as quick as he could. That made me think, although I didn't say anything to Specs at the time, because you couldn't see the egg unless you were standing very close to the clock when the bird came out, and nobody but ourselves had noticed it.

Afternoon school ends at ten to four, and next day Specs and I did a sprint for the study as soon as it was over. Everything had been normal in the dinner hour, but that was three long hours ago. Specs took the cushion cover off the clock, and we stood on each side of it watching and waiting.

Just then Mr Wilde stuck his head into the room. "Oh, McCann," he said, and Specs said, "Yes, sir," and wished he would go away. "You were asking me about the hatching of cuckoos' eggs the other day, remember?" Specs said yes, he remembered. "Well, I've found another book that deals with the subject," said Mr Wilde. Specs was agonised. We could hear the school clock beginning to chime. Mr Wilde heard it too and looked at his watch. "I didn't know it was as late as that," he said, and then, "I say, you've got a cuckoo clock, what a beauty," and he moved up close to look at it. Just then the cuckoo came out and cuckooed, and if Mr Wilde had had his binoculars on he'd have reached for them. The egg was still there, and Mr Wilde saw it. He turned to Specs who was standing watching the clock looking soppy. "McCann," he said, with just the very same expression on his own face. Just for a minute – just for a hair's breadth of a minute – you see, he believed it too. And then of course he was mad with himself, and with us, for he thought the whole thing was a trick on Specs's part to make him look silly. He leaned forward then and prised the little doors open and poked with his finger.

Something small and white and round fell into his hand. He held it to his nose and sniffed, and then put it on our desk and went off without another word.

A little while after he had gone Specs put out rather a shaky hand and picked the thing up. Yes, it was a mothball. He didn't say anything but chucked it out of the window, and we saw it rolling down the pavement and drop into the gutter. Then we got on with our prep.

Tusky came in at the end of the period to borrow a dictionary. He looked rather excited and pleased, but we didn't make any remark and just handed the book over. It was half a minute to five and he hung about looking up his word. Then the doors on the clock opened and the cuckoo came out. "Cuck—" she said, and stopped. For a moment she hung there with her little wings stretched wide, and her bright little eyes looked at Tusky. She knew who'd made a fool of her. Then she went into her house and shut the doors with a tiny vicious bang.

Tusky didn't say a word. He just stood there, looking at the clock and his face got redder and redder. Then he turned and went out. Specs went over to the clock. It was still ticking busily. He bent down close to the little doors. "Thank you, ma'am," he said.

10

Specs's Midsummer Night's Dream

If you've ever seen a copy of our school magazine you'll have noticed a report of the school play and a photograph of the cast. The play was *A Midsummer Night's Dream* by William Shakespeare, and we did it in the school garden on Midsummer Night, that is the 21 of June. I don't know if you've ever heard of the play at all. It's about a lot of people all wandering about at night in a wood near Athens, for one reason or another, and getting mixed up with fairies and magic spells and what not. Not a bit of a likely story, but spots of it are quite funny. The funniest people are some workmen who had gone into the wood to rehearse a play they were to do for the Duke's wedding party. The spot they picked to do their rehearsal was the place where the Fairy Queen was sleeping, so Puck, a kind of fairy message-boy, got rid of them by putting a donkey's head on to one of the workmen so that the others were all terrified and ran away. The one he put the donkey's head on was Bottom the Weaver. That was the part Specs was chosen for, and if you look in the photograph you will see him sitting beside Philpot minor (he was the Fairy Queen, poor lad).

I expect lots of people when they see the photograph will say, "What a pity McCann didn't wear his ass's head! He was the big success of the evening. I'm sure he'd have liked to wear it for the photograph." That's all they know. Wild horses wouldn't have made Specs put his ass's head on for the photograph. And if that sounds funny you'll see what I mean when I tell you what happened.

It was Mr Ellis the English master who was producing the play. He's not a bad soul, just a little bit astray, as if his mind wasn't really on the ball, if you know what I mean. They say he writes, too. He thought it was a wizard idea having the play on Midsummer's Night in the open air – "we may find we have more fairies when we've finished than when we started," he said – that's the kind of man he is. Actually it wasn't a bad idea, because it meant getting off a lot of prep for rehearsals, and it was better sitting about among the trees than at a desk mugging up dates and verbs. He put me down for Hermia, which is a silly part really, but no sillier than lots of the others, and I always have to do a lady's part because I'm not tall. But Specs wasn't a bit pleased when he found he was down to play Bottom the Weaver.

Now Bottom is a wizard part really – all sorts of famous actors have played in it – but of course people will be funny about a thing like an ass's head, saying you'd hardly notice the difference, and that sort of clever business. Not that Specs really minded being ragged, but he just didn't seem to have any enthusiasm for the part. He knew his lines off pat – we'd mugged them up together – but in spite of that he always sounded as if he was just reading them out of the book. Poor Mr Ellis used to get wild with him at rehearsal. "McCann," he would moan, "don't just say the words, try to think what they mean. You're Bottom the Weaver, a rough kind of a customer, rehearsing a play for the Duke's wedding. You're pompous and self-important and bossy, and to crown it all Puck has put an ass's head on your shoulders and the Fairy Queen has fallen madly in love with you. Can't you see that's funny?" Specs would mumble "yessir" in a hopeless kind of way. "Don't you see, McCann, you've got to throw yourself into the part. It isn't enough just to recite your lines – you've got to feel like Bottom the Weaver, and think like him, and *be* him." And Specs would say "yessir" again and rhyme out his next speech like a kindergarten kid giving a recitation. I think if there'd been anyone else to take the part Mr Ellis would have put him in Specs's place, but there wasn't, not in the time, and at least Specs was word perfect.

This was right up to the day before the dress-rehearsal. Now most people had been able to get costumes out of the school wardrobe or borrow them from home (sheets and sandals most of us were wearing), but there were some things that had to be hired: wigs for the ladies for instance and wings for the fairies and for Puck, and of course the ass's head for Bottom. These things didn't come till the Tuesday, and the play was to be on Thursday, with a dress-rehearsal on Wednesday. There was great excitement when these properties arrived. I remember I was trying on my wig – I was an ash-blonde, very fetching – and wondering whether I'd got it on back to front when I heard Specs talking in the queerest kind of way. "I say," he said, "look here." It was the ass's head. "Did you ever see anything like it?" he said, and I certainly never did.

I suppose it must have been made of papier-mâché, because it was so light, and it was beautifully moulded and the outside covered over with grey fur, shaggy and rough. Its eyes were round and golden, with fringed eyelashes, and they shone with a lovely kind of stupid benevolence. The ears were pointed and hairy, and set on at a surprised sort of angle, and the cheeks, just like a real donkey's cheeks, were soft and full. It had the proper kind of wobbly underlip too, and you'd have sworn the black muzzle was damp. It was a grand bit of work – a beautiful bold silly ass. Specs sat and stroked it on his knee, and patted the cheeks and tickled it behind its ears, and it stared back at him with its wide golden eyes.

We used the extra properties that night so as to be used to them before the dress-rehearsal next day. I got my wig slewed round (what I thought was a fringe at the front was really a bun at the back) and we got going. It is surprising what a difference extra properties like this make, but I don't think anybody had any idea of what that ass's head was going to do for Specs. Even before the part of the play where Puck puts the head on him he was acting differently altogether. You'd have thought he knew all of a sudden what sort of a person Bottom was, and what he thought, and how he moved, and what his voice was like. He put all the funny bits across so that he got laughs out of people who had heard the play dozens of times before but had never thought it funny up till then. I saw Mr Ellis shifting about in his seat and giving grunts of surprise and satisfaction. Then, at the place where Bottom goes off-stage in the middle of the rehearsal and comes back again with the ass's head on, everybody really sat up. For Specs was perfect. You see, Bottom didn't know about the ass's head, and he couldn't understand why his friends had run away. He stood there and scratched his head in a way that made you laugh and feel sorry for him at the same time. And when he began to sing a little song to himself to keep up his courage (fancy a donkey singing and you'll know what it was like) the Fairy Queen woke up and fell in love with him, donkey's head and all. People were laughing out loud by this time, and by the time we'd finished Mr Ellis was nearly simmering with excitement.

It wasn't really until the next day that I began to notice the queer things that were happening. I expected Specs to be a bit uppish after the success he'd had, but there was more to it than that. He wasn't only being Bottom the Weaver at rehearsals, he was being him all the time. And not just Bottom the Weaver, but Bottom with the ass's head on. We had stew for dinner, I remember, and in the middle I saw Specs taking a second helping of carrots – piling his plate with them. Now ordinarily Specs doesn't like carrots, but he settled to that plateful as if it were ice cream, and when I said something to him about it he didn't answer but just chewed in a sideways sort of way. And when Hughes said to him, "Specs, you are an ass," Specs didn't punch his nose but actually looked pleased, as if it was a compliment. His voice was different too; he almost brayed. People thought he was doing it for an act, but I knew he wasn't, because I went down to the post office with him after dinner hour, and he brayed at the girl for a couple of stamps till she looked quite scared. Coming home he kept picking pieces of hay off the hedge where it had been left by a passing cart, and he put them in his mouth and chewed them; he didn't spit them out either, because I watched.

The dress-rehearsal was a terrific success. When Bottom was on stage people simply laughed and laughed until they cried, and some of the staff who popped in to see how it was going along stayed to watch it through and they laughed as loudly as anyone. We were let off school the afternoon before the actual performance, with the idea that we had a rest. It was a wonderful day – not a breath of wind and the sun was hot in a clear blue sky. It was really too hot to do anything much, and I thought I'd hang around and keep an eye on Specs, for to be honest I was worried about him. He wandered around after dinner and wouldn't say where he wanted to go or what he wanted to do, and I had the funny idea that he was trying to give me the slip, so I cleared off and when he thought I wasn't there I came back and did a spot of sleuthing to find out what he was really up to.

As soon as he thought I wasn't watching he set off at a kind of a canter – yes, it was like that – for the hayfield above the cricket pitch. There's an old donkey that lives in the field up there. Sandbag, we call him. He used to help McIvor the groundsman with cutting and rolling the pitch before we had the motor mower, and with other jobs around the place, but now he's too old, and we're mechanised anyhow, so he just browses about in the paddock and never takes much interest in anybody. Not as a rule, that is. But this afternoon it was different. As soon as Specs came into the field Sandbag pricked up his ears and came running to him, and they stood close together as if they were talking for a long time. I stood at the gate watching them. Just then Mr Ellis came past on one of his country walks and he stopped beside me and looked over the gate too. There were Specs and Sandbag cheek to cheek. "Ha," said Mr Ellis, but in rather an odd sort of voice I thought, "our young friend has come for some tips." "Yes, sir," I said, and even at the time I thought it was rather bright of me, "tips from the ass's mouth." Mr Ellis laughed out loud at this and went on with his walk, and Specs heard and saw me, and came over looking cross, and wouldn't speak to me all the way back to school.

It was a wonderful evening for the show. We started at eight o'clock, you see, when the evening was just beginning, and the wood at the end of the garden really looked like a magic kind of wood, all shadowy and mysterious. There were some foxgloves growing in it, and the last of the bluebells, and as the evening darkened hidden lights lit up in the trees, and somehow it didn't seem at all surprising to see fairies and dukes and Athenian ladies and a gang of theatrical workmen all going about their business in the school garden. There was a sort of spell on everything. The audience felt if too. There wasn't a cough or a fidget out of them. They felt everything we meant them to feel, and some more that we hadn't thought of ourselves up till then, though William Shakespeare must have thought of it when he wrote it. I know we all acted better than ever before, but best of all was Bottom the Weaver – Specs McCann. Each time he came on you could feel the audience leaning a little bit nearer, and after it was over they clapped and shouted for him – and for all of us – till we were tired of bowing and smiling.

We had a wizard supper party afterwards in the dining-room, and after that we were all so tired we just fell upstairs and into bed, with the greasepaint more on than off. I had been keeping a little out of Specs's way through the evening, because he took such a dim view of my spying on him in the afternoon, and it was only when I was in bed that I looked over at him in the bed next to mine. And do you know – he had gone to bed ass's head and all! I know we were all playing the fool till the last, and he must have just fallen asleep without taking it off. Anyhow, there he lay looking so silly in his striped pyjamas, with the big ass's head on the pillow, snoring ever so faintly down the wide nostrils. Some of the other chaps were giggling, but they thought it was just an act and everyone was tired so they soon settled down. But I couldn't settle. The window beside our beds was open, and it was all silvery and moonlit outside, and – though everyone had gone home long ago somehow I had the feeling that the garden wasn't empty. It was full of voices and magic. Mr Ellis was right – there were other fairies. So I lay and listened to the Midsummer-Night garden talking, and tried not to worry about Specs.

And then someone came in through the open window from the garden. I couldn't see who it was, but I felt him. And just like at the end of the play when Puck was undoing the magic, he lifted the ass's head off Specs's shoulders, and I heard him saying, "Now when thou wak'st with thine own fool's eyes peep." And then someone laughed and set the head at the foot of the bed and went out into the garden again.

Next morning we were all tired and browned off. But brownest of us all was Specs. When he woke up and saw the ass's head grinning at him from the end of the bed he growled "Thank goodness that thing is going back where it came from to-day; it gives me the willies." And when we were all called for a photograph in the middle of the morning, nothing Mr Ellis or anyone else said would persuade him to wear the thing – so that's why he hasn't got it on.

Mr Ellis is talking of doing *The Merchant of Venice* next year. He says Specs would make a wonderful Shylock. I don't think much of the idea, do you?

11

Specs's Uncle Ephraim

We were both surprised when there was a letter for Specs in the post on Wednesday. His mother's letter always comes on Mondays, and his sisters used to write on Fridays till he managed to get them stopped. I pretended not to notice the letter because we'd had a row about something or other in the dorm, and weren't speaking to each other any more just then. But I watched Specs round the corner of my porridge spoon, and I saw that what was in the letter seemed to surprise him even more. You could nearly hear his eyes popping. "Here," he said at last, "I've had a letter from my uncle that's in Australia – he's in Belfast." "I thought you said he was in Australia," I said. After all, I have my pride. "That's where he lives, you loon," Specs said, "but he's over here on business, and he says can we meet him in Belfast this evening." "We?" I asked, still a little icy. "Well, anyone," Specs said offhand, "it doesn't matter who. It's me he's coming to see, but he says bring anyone along." Now this was difficult. Of course I wanted to go, but I didn't want to look over-anxious, and Specs didn't want to seem as if he cared whether I went or not. "What's he like, your Uncle What's-his-name?" I asked, to gain time. Specs squinted at the letter. "It looks like 'Ephraim'." "Don't you know your own uncle's name?" "I've never seen him; he went to Australia when he was twelve, and mother calls him Curly," he explained. "Ephraim – gosh!" I said. "It's in the Bible," Specs said, crossly. "I know, but gosh!" "Well, are you coming or aren't you?" he asked. I thought I could accept now. "I may as well," I said. I think Specs was as glad as I was to have things straight again without any bother. "Uncle Ephraim says he's written to the Head as well, so it should be all right," he said. "Ephraim," I murmured, chewing it over, "Ephraim – it's quite a name." "I expect he's quite a chap," said Specs.

Well, the headmaster – that's my father – gave us permission to go, so after prep that evening Specs and I set off. We were missing Mr Thomas's Madrigal Society, so we felt no matter how dreary Uncle Ephraim might be, he had his points. We could hear the choir piping up on the first item just as we went down the drive. "Oh who will o'er the lea with me?" trilled Specs, sprinting as he saw a bus coming round the corner, and we were still "nonny-no-ing" and "derry-down-derrying" when we climbed on board. One old lady looked rather nervous.

We were to meet Uncle Ephraim under the clock at the GPO in Royal Avenue, so we couldn't very well miss him, or at least he couldn't very well miss us. "I wonder what he'll be like," I said. "A big wide hat and shiny yellow shoes," Specs suggested. "A check shirt and a ring on his little finger," I added. "Do you suppose he'll chew gum?" "No," said Specs, "but he'll roll his own cigarettes, and blow smoke rings that go through each other." We went on with this all the way in the bus, as if we were playing the "Minister's Cat" and were quite surprised when we got to the post-office corner, and nobody was standing under the clock. There was a prosperous white cat sitting there washing herself, but she moved further up the street when we arrived and went on with her washing. There was no sign yet of Uncle Ephraim. Of course it was only twelve minutes to, so we spent the time watching the people coming past and trying to guess which would be him. At first it was fun, but after a while it got a bit boring, specially when several people we thought might be him just went on past, talking and laughing and hurrying – they had all somewhere to go. Then the white cat finished washing and went off on her business, looking at us a little pityingly. I began to feel anxious, and so did Specs, though neither of us said so till afterwards. We turned round to have one more squint at the clock – it was five and three-quarter minutes past six by now – when a horn hooted noisily. There was a taxi drawn up at the kerb, and the door of it was standing open. A big man was leaning out. "Come on, you fellows," he said, "we've got to get moving."

We didn't see Uncle Ephraim till we were in the taxi and had actually driven off, and even then it was a bit dark and hard to make him out very distinctly, but but by bit we checked up on him, and he fitted exactly to our guess, all of it – yellow shiny shoes, check shirt, even the gold signet ring. And I never saw anyone roll cigarettes so elegantly, or blow such lovely smoke rings as Specs's Uncle Ephraim.

We must have stared at him rather a lot, but he didn't seem to notice; he was leaning forward talking to the driver through the little glass panel, and it was then I noticed that the taxi was travelling more than ordinarily fast, and that Uncle Ephraim was urging the driver to go faster still. "There he is," he said, through the panel, "he'll turn right up here." And then, "That's him – on the far side of that bus – step on it," and the driver of the taxi stepped. By this time we were out of the centre of the city and into a hive of side streets I didn't know. Uncle Ephraim took time then to turn round and say to us, "Glad you fellows could come along." "It was nice of you to ask us," said Specs; "I suppose you're over here on business." Uncle Ephraim grinned. "That's it in the car in front," he said, and turned again to the road ahead, and blew six smoke rings quickly one through the other down the driver's neck. We were as keen on the chase as he was by now, although of course we didn't know what in the world it was all about. It was a sleek black car we were following, like an elongated slug, but could it move? And I never knew a man handle a taxi like our driver did. The black car streaked on, always half a street ahead, and we rattled and bumped after it – up one road – down the next, twice round a roundabout – and never let it out of our sight.

Then to our surprise we came to a part of Belfast I did know, quite well. Up the Stranmillis Road it was, and the black car actually turned in at the Museum and drew up. "You've got him now, Uncle Ephraim," Specs hissed (he really did hiss it) and our taxi drew alongside, wheezing but triumphant. A man got out of the black car; he didn't look at us at all, but locked the car carefully and went into the Museum. An unhealthy type he was, shiny black hair and a dark hat, you know.

Uncle Ephraim didn't move; he just sat there. "Aren't you going to pick him up?" Specs asked. He shook his head. "Not till he takes me somewhere worthwhile," said Uncle Ephraim, "this don't teach me anything." And then he said, "You get along after him – he doesn't know you – and keep your eye on him for me. He's gone in there to get his breath and have a quick think. He knows he's in a spot, and we'll keep him in it. Follow him round, and if he acts suspicious come on out and tell me."

We were after the man right away, and ran him to earth among the old bicycles and spinning-wheels. Then we put in the queerest evening I remember. The man went from room to room, and we followed him, always a little way behind. He didn't take long on the ground floor, but as soon as we were up on the first floor he started his tricks, doubling back on himself into a room he'd already been in – running from one floor to the next and then turning directly he was there and coming down again. One time we thought he'd given us the slip, but then we saw he was standing between two dummies in uniform, very still, so that he looked like an exhibit himself. And in the room where the cases of birds' eggs were he pretended to tie his shoelace and then, still bent double like that, crept to the end of the showcase and made for the door. You could tell he wasn't really looking at the exhibits. He didn't even slacken pace in front of the Irish wolfhound. I was sorry it couldn't put its head out through the glass and take a bit off his leg. I suppose he expected Uncle Ephraim would be following him, but after a little while he found that there was always one or other of us at one or other end of the corridor, and it must have dawned on him that we were working together. Then he gave a very loud and disgusted grunt, and ran down the stairs very quickly and out to his car.

We piled into the taxi, and the chase began again, while we told Uncle Ephraim what had happened in the Museum. "Stout fellows," was all he said, but it felt like getting a medal.

This time the black car made straight for the centre of the city and stopped at a lighted doorway. "Well," said Uncle Ephraim, "looks like he's going to eat. After all, he's human. I'm hungry too – come on, chaps, what are we waiting for?" None of that coy business about schoolboys' appetites, you know – just "Come on, chaps" and a wave of the hand. Soon we were sitting down studying a menu, and a couple of tables away the man we were following was lowering soup. He didn't look up at Uncle Ephraim as we came past, and when we sat down he pretended to read a paper, but Uncle Ephraim sat staring straight at him, and blowing smoke rings, one through the other.

I don't remember when I ate a meal like that – it was a man's meal, and were we ready for it? I'd never been in that café before – Specs says it wasn't the kind of place you'd call a café, more like an "eating-house", whatever he means by that – and I was afraid the man would get up and leave just when we started the fried chicken and peas and we'd have to get up and leave too. Of course, I could have left, right away – Uncle Ephraim was that kind of person – but I was glad I didn't have to all the same, and it was exciting never knowing when you started a course whether you'd get to the end of it or not. I had just put down my spoon after my *Pêche Melba*

– that's ice cream with fruit and nuts and all sorts of trimmings – and decided that if the man got up to go now I didn't mind, when Specs looked at his watch and we found it was twenty past nine. Well, our bus went at half-past, and we had to be on it. We explained this to Uncle Ephraim, and he took it very well. "I know how it is," he said, "you can't help these things. Glad to have had you with me. Buzz off now. I'll be seeing you." So we made a bolt for it, but we turned at the door and waved to Uncle Ephraim, and he waved back at us and grinned. "I wish we could have stayed," said Specs, "I'd like to have been in at the kill. But gosh, what an evening!"

We were feeling rather full of righteousness as well as of food when we turned in at school, and it surprised us to be told in the hall that the Head was waiting to see us. He was sitting in his study, looking tough. "Well?" he asked, "had a pleasant evening?" Specs was in such a rosy haze the sarcasm went past him, and he said, "Oh, sir, and how!" "I'm glad you enjoyed it," my father said, and even Specs didn't miss the tone this time, "a telegram came for you after you went out." We didn't say anything, it seemed safer. My father took up the telegram and read it out. "Sorry for change of plans. Will meet you and friend tomorrow evening instead, same time. Uncle Edward."

We both gasped. "Uncle who?" said Specs. "Your Uncle Edward, of course," said my father, handing the wire across the desk. Specs looked at it and swallowed, and said "Yes."

Matron came in just then to say Hughes was 104 now and it looked like a measles rash but you never know with measles do you, and we were never so glad to see Matron in our lives. Father, that is the Head, told us we could meet Uncle Edward tomorrow, as it was good of him to make the arrangement, but that we were gated on Saturdays, till the end of term. It was bad enough, but we felt it could have been a great deal worse.

When we got to the clock next evening the cat was there again, and it looked very surprised to see us. Uncle Edward was a mild little man in a bowler hat and a waterproof. He took us to see a rather unfunny film, and then we had tea at a café where all the things we wanted were just off. He kept apologising though it wasn't his fault, and we didn't know what to say to put it right. He sat and smoked messily at a cigarette out of a packet, and asked Specs lots of family questions that Specs didn't know the answers to. We caught a bus before the one we meant to and came back to school early.

We didn't talk about Uncle Ephraim. Perhaps that seems odd, but really both of us felt so queer about it – who could he have been? Why did he stop his taxi to pick us up? Why was he following the black car, and – oh, half a hundred other why's. Specs just said one thing. He said, "I hope he got what he wanted from that unhealthy type," and I said "Yes."

It was very dull on Saturday afternoons for the rest of term, not being able to leave the school grounds. We didn't know what to do. Sometimes, just for the sake of not doing nothing we went to the first form film shows. These were for the very young boys who couldn't get home on Saturdays. We used to slip in at the back when the show had started and out again as it was finishing, so I don't think anyone noticed. I was glad it was dark;

Specs looked so funny, what I could see of him, all doubled up on one of their small chairs, looking out at the screen through his knees. Most of the pictures were educational or documentary, cotton picking, sheep rearing, deep sea fishing, you know the kind of thing. One Saturday there was one about cattle farming in Australia; the usual stuff, lots of lowing herds and galloping horses, and wide open spaces and dust. I must say those men on horseback knew how to handle their horses and their cattle. There was a nice fade-out to it too. A big man riding away from us into the sunset, and just – *just* as he was getting near the skyline he stopped his horse and turned, and the camera took a close-up of him. And do you know, it was Uncle Ephraim, every long inch of him, and he waved and grinned at us as if to say "Hallo, you chaps," and we grinned and waved back.